Praise for *The Friends of Harry Perkins*

'Terrific ... measured, heart-stopping, moving, clear-eyed.' Stephen Frears

'Brilliant, chilling and all too plausible.' Alastair Campbell

'A very knowledgeable and pleasurable political thriller.' Mark Lawson, *The Guardian*

'Faced with the horrors of Brexit and a Conservative government overrun by dubious right-wingers ... the beleaguered one-nation wing of the Tory party and even the tabloid press appear suddenly as a force for good. One of the tantalising questions is whether they are really out to help ...' Robert Shrimsley, *Financial Times*

'Brexit has been a catastrophic failure ... Trying to undo it means confronting all the pent up frustration that led to Brexit in the first place. This produces the deepest irony of all, and the one that gives the novel its peculiar bite ...' David Runciman, *London Review of Books*

'Readable and very entertaining, and should appeal to both sides of the divide.' *The Spectator*

'The friends of Chris Mullin – and they are legion at Westminster – have been eagerly awaiting this book and they will not be disappointed. A brilliant, topical sequel to *A Very British Coup.*' Andrew Adonis, *The House*

'Briskly paced ... spartan ... and most affecting.' *Irish Times*

'Excellent ... a worthy sequel to a true classic of political fiction.' Matthew d'Ancona

'Mullin has the knack of pithy description, adding touches of colour and wit.' *Glasgow Herald*

THE
FRIENDS
OF HARRY
PERKINS

CHRIS MULLIN

SCRIBNER

LONDON NEW YORK SYDNEY TORONTO NEW DELHI

First published in Great Britain by Scribner, an imprint of
Simon & Schuster UK Ltd, 2019
This edition published by Scribner, an imprint of
Simon & Schuster UK Ltd, 2020
A CBS COMPANY

Copyright © Chris Mullin, 2019

SCRIBNER and design are registered trademarks of The Gale Group, Inc.,
used under licence by Simon & Schuster Inc.

The right of Chris Mullin to be identified as author of
this work has been asserted in accordance with the
Copyright, Designs and Patents Act, 1988.

3 5 7 9 10 8 6 4 2

Simon & Schuster UK Ltd
1st Floor
222 Gray's Inn Road
London WC1X 8HB

www.simonandschuster.co.uk
www.simonandschuster.com.au
www.simonandschuster.co.in

Simon & Schuster Australia, Sydney
Simon & Schuster India, New Delhi

A CIP catalogue record for this book is available from the British Library

Paperback ISBN: 978-1-4711-8250-1
eBook ISBN: 978-1-4711-8249-5
eAudio ISBN: 978-1-4711-8375-1

Typeset in Palatino by M Rules
Printed and bound by CPI Group (UK) Ltd, Croydon CR0 4YY

MIX
Paper from
responsible sources
FSC® C020471

IN MEMORY OF THE LATE JO COX MP

CONTENTS

PREFACE

Many times in the nearly forty years since *A Very British Coup* was first published I have been asked if I planned to write a sequel. For most of that time I had no such plan, but here it is. As with its predecessor, *The Friends of Harry Perkins* is set in the near future in a political landscape that will be recognisable to anyone familiar with contemporary politics. An air of pessimism prevails. Post-Brexit Britain is not a happy place although, contrary to what some predicted, there has been no great Armageddon, just a long slow decline into insularity and irrelevance. As for the Labour Party, I regret to report that it has been in opposition for as long as anyone can remember. Charismatic leadership is urgently required. Enter Fred Thompson, a veteran of an earlier era.

The fact that Thompson turns out to be a pragmatist will be a disappointment to some. There are many in the Labour movement who prefer glorious defeats to the messy realities of victory. Had I known that Thompson was going to rise again from the ashes of the Perkins' administration, I'd have given him a more memorable name. Suffice to say, as readers of the earlier work will know, Thompson, a former journalist, cut his teeth as a political adviser and confidant of Perkins and was present at The Fall. He married Elizabeth Fain, the daughter of an earl and a former equerry to the king, with no shortage of contacts in the secret world. After the fall of Perkins, the young couple moved away to the Western Isles where Thompson was last heard of scratching a living working for the *West Highland Free Press*.

I had better mention, before someone else does, that as regards chronology a slight leap of imagination is required. *A Very British Coup* was set in the late 1980s and it is stretching the imagination somewhat to imagine that the movers and shakers of that era would still be active in politics today. Thompson himself would be in his mid-sixties, whereas here I would guess he is no more than about forty. Likewise Joan Cook and Jock Steeples, sole survivors of the ill-fated Perkins government, are unlikely to have remained active long enough to feature in a Thompson shadow cabinet. On this I must ask the readers' forbearance.

Two other veterans of the earlier work are worthy of

mention. Molly Spence, wife of the managing director of British Insulated Fuels, the company responsible for the near meltdown of the Windermere nuclear reactor. Her affair with Perkins was used to blackmail him into resignation. Finally, of course, there is the shadowy Sir Peregrine Craddock, architect of the coup which brought down the Perkins government. Although now long retired and increasingly frail, Sir Peregrine is, as we shall see, still a man of influence.

A Very British Coup has endured so long because a number of the events described were subsequently shown to be true. There *was* an M15 agent on the council of the Campaign for Nuclear Disarmament. The security service *was* vetting senior BBC personnel. And in 1987 a senior M15 officer, Peter Wright, caused a sensation with his claim that a group of M15 officers, of whom he was one, had plotted to undermine the government of Harold Wilson. Suddenly the possibility that the Establishment might conspire to bring down an elected government no longer seemed so remote. With the rise of Jeremy Corbyn, accompanied by warnings from a former head of M16 that his election would be 'profoundly dangerous for the nation', the subject is suddenly topical again. The publishers of *A Very British Coup* are cunningly marketing the latest edition as 'the novel that foretold the rise of Corbyn' and it has been reprinted several times in the last two years.

Harry Perkins, a former Sheffield steelworker, was brilliantly brought to life by that great actor Ray McAnally in the award-winning television series based on the novel. Fred Thompson is a less colourful character, but as we shall see he too is a man whose hour has come. Or has it? Now read on.

Chris Mullin, December 2018

ONE

Harry Perkins was buried on the day that America declared war on China.

He was seen off in style. Sheffield City Council declared three days of mourning. His coffin, draped in the banner of his old trade union branch, lay in state in the vestibule of the City Hall. By the end of the third day, an estimated 50,000 people had filed past. His request to be buried with 'no flowers, no fuss' was cheerfully ignored. Floral tributes lined the steps. People waited patiently in line to pass the coffin, straining to read the messages. Journalists amused themselves speculating about the origin of some of the anonymous wreaths. *'All my love, M. x'*, was widely held to be from Molly Spence, the woman whose affair with Perkins lit the long fuse that led to his downfall. Most interest, however, focused on a bouquet of white lilies bearing a handwritten message, *'To Harry*

Perkins, with affection and respect', followed by scrawled initials. The first letter was clearly a P, but the rest was illegible. Enquiry revealed that the order for the lilies had been placed in Somerset and the evidence pointed to Sir Peregrine Craddock. Nothing had been heard of Sir Peregrine for years (not that much was heard of him at any time during his long and distinguished career of public service). He would now be in his late eighties. Calls to his home, a Jacobean pile somewhat in need of renovation, were answered by an elderly woman who stated gruffly that Sir Peregrine was unavailable. Nothing new there. Sir Peregrine had never been available. Even now, nearly ten years after the momentous events that crowned his career and abruptly ended that of Harry Perkins, Sir Peregrine's memoirs would have fetched a small fortune. There was no sign, however, that the great man had committed his version of events to paper. He remained discreet to the end.

Perkins was buried on a cold, clear day in February. By special resolution the city council unanimously decreed that the General Cemetery be reopened so that he could be laid to rest among Sheffield's greatest sons. A space was found for him under a weeping ash, near the grave of the Chartist Samuel Holberry, one of Perkins' few heroes. The crowds who followed his coffin were greater even than those who had followed Holberry's. 'Harry Perkins,' said one commentator, 'was probably the last hero the British working classes will ever produce.'

In death, Perkins attracted a much friendlier press than he had done in life. Those who had most reviled him were most fulsome in their tributes. 'Honourable to his fingertips,' said *The Times*. The *Sun* filled its front page with a flattering portrait taken on the night of his greatest triumph, alongside the headline, 'Goodbye, Harry, We'll Miss You'. So far as anyone could recall it was the only friendly reference to Perkins that had ever appeared in the *Sun*. 'A giant among pygmies,' said a leader in the *Mail*. It went on, 'In an age of Labour politicians who would run a mile at the mention of nuclear disarmament or come over faint at the whisper of the word "socialism", we pay tribute to a man who stuck to his principles to the end . . .'

Everyone who had loved Harry Perkins came to see him off. And so did some who had not. Lawrence Wainwright, who briefly displaced him as prime minister, was there. His presence near the head of the procession provoked low hissing from some sections of the crowd. Jock Steeples, a wise old owl, now in his late seventies but still active in parliament, marched the whole way. His craggy features instantly recognisable. Joan Cook, the firebrand who had once been home secretary, was there too, immaculate as ever. Alongside her was Perkins' loyal sidekick, Fred Thompson, who with his posh young wife, Elizabeth Fain,

7

had disappeared to a croft in the Western Isles where he grew vegetables and scratched a living writing for a local newspaper. He was also an occasional columnist and book reviewer in the national press.

But what really made the funeral of Harry Perkins a truly extraordinary event was the attendance, in defiance of protocol and much official advice, of the king. Escorted only by a single detective, His Majesty had appeared, unannounced, as the procession left Barker's Pool. He paused to shake hands with the mayor and other dignitaries and then, without ceremony, took his place at the head of the official party.

***

Later, much later, Jock Steeples, Joan Cook and Fred Thompson repaired to the Parkside Working Men's Club where they were joined by Perkins' agent, Vera Clarke.

'Fancy His Majesty showing up,' said Thompson. 'That was a turn-up for the books.'

'Aye,' said Steeples. 'The king always had a soft spot for Harry. Plus he no doubt felt bad about what happened. If he'd put his foot down, Harry might well have survived.'

'Surprising that Harry stayed on at Westminster,' remarked Mrs Cook.

'Sad truth is,' said Thompson quietly, 'he had nowhere else to go. No hinterland, you see. Didn't read much. No woman. Not since Molly, any rate. Fancied himself as a gardener, but never really got round to it and in the end his health wasn't up to it.'

'And of course there is no way he could have gone to the Lords, along with the rest of the great and the good,' said Mrs Cook.

'Offered a peerage, but he turned it down. "Too young to die," he said.'

'But of course he did die,' said Mrs Cook ruefully, 'that's why we're here.'

'Truth is,' said Steeples, 'he never really recovered from the manner of his downfall. Knocked the stuffing out of him, it did. Self-confidence just drained away.'

'He gave in too easily,' said Mrs Cook.

'Aye, that he did. And he knew it, too. Never forgave himself.'

They talked of war with China. 'Thank goodness that lunatic Trump is no longer in charge,' remarked Steeples. 'He'd have been the death of all of us.'

'With any luck,' said Thompson, 'it will all calm down in a few days.'

'Don't count on it, son,' said Steeples.

He paused to watch a news clip of the funeral on the widescreen television at far end of the bar. 'Fancy that snake Wainwright showing his face,' said Thompson as the camera briefly alighted upon the face of Perkins' nemesis.

'Looks distinctly uneasy.'

'As well he might.'

'No sign of him at the reception.'

'Just as well he didn't hang around. There might have been an incident.'

'Changing the subject,' said Vera, 'who is going to replace Harry? There will be a by-election and we need a decent candidate.'

'You'll need a good local man,' said Steeples. 'Or woman,' he added hastily, with a sideways glance at Mrs Cook.

'Better move fast, before central casting imposes some upwardly mobile young android.'

'The problem is, we haven't got anyone. A couple of councillors fancy themselves, but neither is fit to fill Harry's shoes.'

'How about a decent trade unionist? Surely there's still one or two of them about.'

'The unions are a shadow of what they used to be in the days when we had steel and engineering. Nowadays it's all shopping malls and zero-hours contracts. Only the public services are still unionised and half their branches are in the hands of headbanging Trots.'

Steeples' eyes lit up. 'There is one obvious solution: young Fred here.'

'You're joking.'

'Why not? You're a figure of substance. You've got – or at least you had until you moved away to that darn island – a national profile. Plus you were Harry's right-hand man. You're his natural successor. You'd be a shoo-in.'

***

A statement from the foreign ministry in Beijing said that the People's Republic of China would not be intimidated by warlike noises emanating from Washington. China intended to reclaim territory that was rightfully hers, starting with the Diayou islands, 'illegally occupied' by the Japanese. After which she would turn her attention to the Paracels claimed by Vietnam and then to the 'long overdue' liberation of Taiwan.

Two

An unmade track leading down to a sandy bay. A white-washed stone house, solar panels on the roof. Shirts fluttering on a clothes line strung between a wooden post and the corner of an outhouse. Logs stacked neatly against the porch wall. Outside, evidence of children: a tricycle, a football, a rag doll sitting on a low wall by a bed of leeks. Beyond the garden, through a wooden gate, a path leading down to the beach where a small boat is moored. By the house, a battered red Volvo splashed with mud, a model no longer in production. Across the bay, more houses, also whitewashed. Ribbons of smoke rising from chimneys.

Elizabeth was in the kitchen, back to the Aga, hands on hips, a dishcloth over her shoulder and wearing a red apron across the front of which was the slogan, 'Keep Calm and Carry On'.

* * *

'You must be mad,' she said.

The years had been kind to Elizabeth. The island climate suited her. She had acquired a light tan, a sprinkling of freckles on her cheeks, a slightly fuller figure, one or two lines around the eyes, but was otherwise unblemished. Accent still unmistakably Home Counties, but no longer Chelsea. She still displayed the same infectious smile that had once drawn Fred to her. No longer a party girl, she had adapted well to motherhood, marriage and island living.

Thompson, lately arrived back from Sheffield, bag still unpacked in the hall, had just announced that he proposed to apply for the Labour nomination for Parkside.

'After all we've been through. I thought you'd done with bloody politics.'

'It's what Harry would have wanted.'

'Never mind Harry. He's beyond caring. What about me and the girls? Or didn't you think of asking?'

'Of course I was going to ask.'

'What did you say to Jock Steeples?'

'That I would think about it.'

'Well, now you can tell him you have thought about it and decided against.'

* * *

That evening, after the children were in bed and the dishes cleared, Thompson returned to the subject. 'For goodness' sake, Lizzie. How long do you think we can stay here?'

'What do you mean?'

'Look at us. Barely scraping a living. Our savings, such as they were, have gone. My work is running out. Your parents have been generous, but we can't rely on them for ever. Sooner or later I'm going to have to find a job in the real world.'

'The children are happy.' This, said quietly. As though she knew he had a point. 'They'll be fine.'

'And then what? The nearest secondary school is two ferry rides away. Either they'll have to board or we'll have to move.'

* * *

'Daddy, why was Mummy shouting last night?' asked Catherine. They were sitting on a grassy mound above the beach, seal watching. Lucy was splashing in a nearby rock pool.

'We had a little disagreement.'

'What about?'

'I have been offered a job, in Sheffield.'

'Where's Sheffield?'

'A long way away.'

'You're not going to leave us, are you, Daddy?' A cloud passed across that radiant face.

'No, of course not, darling.'

'There's a boy in my class called Calum whose father went to work in England and never came back.'

'I'll never, never leave you.' He put his arm around her and held her close.

'Promise?'

'I promise.'

* * *

Later, after two days of uncomfortable silence. 'If ... *if* ... we were to go back, where would we live?'

'I don't know. Either London or Sheffield.'

'*Sheffield?*'

'These days MPs are expected to live in their constituencies.'

'In some 1960s tower block, I suppose.'

'Of course not. We can do better than that. A house with a garden.'

'And the schools?'

'At least as good as here.'

* * *

On the fifth day Elizabeth conceded. 'Okay, Fred. If that's what you really want.'

'It is, Lizzie. It is. The alternative is a lifetime with nothing useful to do.'

He held out his arms and they embraced.

* * *

So it was agreed. If he was selected, they would move to Sheffield. Renting, at first. If Elizabeth and the children didn't settle, they would move to London, leaving Fred to commute. Elizabeth's parents owned the flat in Chelsea where she had been living when she first met Thompson. No doubt they would allow her to reclaim it. For the time being, they would hang on to the croft and use it as a holiday home. Hopefully that would put paid to any withdrawal symptoms.

Next day Thompson rang Jock Steeples with the news.

'In that case you'd better get yourself down to Sheffield, sharpish. Events move fast in by-elections. There's already half a dozen hopefuls snooping around, including a bright young fellow from central casting, fluent in the slogans of the hour. He's the one you'll have to watch.'

Within two hours, Thompson was on a ferry to the

mainland. By late evening he was closeted with half a dozen local movers and shakers in a back room at the Parkside Working Men's Club. 'We thought you'd given up on us,' said Vera. 'What took you so long?'

Thompson explained about Elizabeth.

'And has she come round?'

'I think so, yes.'

'If elected, are you going to live here? That's the first question you'll be asked.'

'That's the plan, yes.'

'One other fly in the ointment. There's talk of head office imposing a candidate. They can do that at by-elections. We've told them that people up here won't stand for it, but I wouldn't put it past them zealots in London to trample all over us.'

Vera Clarke was a no-nonsense woman of indeterminate age. Such women are the lifeblood of almost every constituency association in the country, regardless of party. Fiercely loyal, relentlessly parochial and always on the side of the established order, whatever the established order might be. It just so happened that in Parkside for as long as anyone could remember the established order was Harry Perkins which meant that Mrs Clarke (she was a Mrs though no one could ever remember seeing a Mr) was not quite as parochial as her counterparts elsewhere.

'Our best hope of heading off an imposed candidate is Mrs Cook,' said Ronnie Morgan. Ronnie and Harry went back a long way. They had both served apprenticeships at the Firth Brown special steels plant, both been shop stewards and it was Ronnie who had first encouraged Harry to put his name in for the Parkside nomination when the seat fell vacant. He was a keeper of the flame. 'We've been on to her this lunchtime. Pointed out that if they are not careful they'll end up with someone local standing as an independent who might just win. It's happened before. No threats, like. We just pointed out the realities. Mrs Cook says it's touch and go. We'll find out tomorrow.'

* * *

In the event, the national executive backed off and decided to allow an open selection. No more was heard of the bright young man from London who had no doubt decided to offer his services in more promising territory. A timetable was published. The selection would take place in ten days.

There followed a week of door-knocking, during which Fred was introduced by his small band of supporters to as many members of the Parkside Labour Party as could be located. By and large the natives were friendly, though there was some scepticism that any long-haired southern intellectual, even one who lived on an island in Scotland and had been so close to the much-loved Harry, could hope to represent the people of a close-knit northern stronghold such as this. To every such doubter Fred responded with one of Harry's favourite aphorisms, 'It's not where you come from that matters, it's where you're going to.' But he did take the precaution of getting a haircut.

The selection took place on a cold Saturday afternoon in the oak-panelled council chamber of Sheffield Town Hall. The other four shortlisted candidates consisted of two councillors (one a woman), a young trade union official and a former minister who had lost his seat in the massacre that followed two dismal years of Lawrence Wainwright's government. All save the young trade unionist claimed a close relationship with Harry. All spoke warmly of his legacy (although in truth his legacy was high hopes followed by resounding defeat) and all promised to honour his memory. The final ballot came down to a choice between Fred Thompson and the former minister. Thompson won comfortably.

The by-election was set for three weeks hence. 'A word of advice, son,' whispered Ronnie Morgan in the club that evening. 'Always remember that all the instincts of the working classes are conservative. On race, patriotism, the bomb, Brexit – you name it. It's just that they happen to vote Labour.'

Brexit Britain was a gloomy place. True, the Armageddon that some had prophesied had not occurred, but neither had the economic miracle promised by the Brexiteers. The value of the pound had fallen steadily against the euro, the dollar and the yuan. The much-vaunted increase in trade with the Commonwealth had not materialised. The Americans, too, were proving particularly obstreperous. Even now, after nearly a decade of negotiations, no significant agreements had been reached. At the UN there was talk of relieving the UK of its seat on the Security Council.

* * *

In Washington it was announced that the president had ordered the Pacific Fleet into the waters off the coast of Japan. In Tokyo the prime minister announced that Japanese forces would fight to the last man to prevent a Chinese takeover of even one square centimetre of his country's sovereign territory. In Beijing chanting crowds laid siege to the Japanese and US embassies.

THREE

Fred Thompson was returned as member of parliament for Sheffield Parkside on a rainy day in March. Indeed it had rained for most of March. The only evidence of spring was a few bedraggled daffodils in the patch of grass opposite the Parkside Working Men's Club. Although the name of Harry Perkins was much invoked, voter turnout was disappointing, with the result that Harry's majority more than halved. The good news was that the Tory lost his deposit and the UKIP candidate polled less than the Monster Raving Loony Party. The natural order of British politics appeared to be reasserting itself.

'Don't take it personally, son,' said Ronnie Morgan as they picked their way dejectedly through the election debris after the declaration. 'Fact is, you're there for life now. Unless,' he added, 'you do something stupid.'

Elizabeth had parked the children with her parents in

Oxfordshire and joined Fred for the last week of the campaign. They found lodgings in a Hallam B & B. The owner was a Liberal Democrat, but it didn't matter since there wasn't an election in Hallam. Fred worried that Elizabeth was too posh for Parkside, but she mucked in without complaint and the locals soon warmed to her.

* * *

He was sworn in on a Wednesday, immediately after Prime Minister's Questions amid some resounding (and so far as some were concerned, a mite hypocritical) hear-hearing from the opposition benches and ironic cheering from the Tory side. 'Son of Harry,' shouted one of the Tories. 'Grandson, more likely,' cried a voice from the opposition benches. The speaker shook his hand warmly and wished him well. He was proposed and seconded by Jock Steeples and Mrs Cook. Elizabeth and the children were in the gallery.

Afterwards he entertained the family to tea on the terrace, while the children amused themselves waving to the people on the passing tourist boats.

'Daddy,' said Catherine, aged eight and three quarters. She had her mother's blue eyes and fair hair.

'Yes, my sunshine.'

'Do all men go to parliament?'

'Only those who are elected'

'And women, too, darling,' Elizabeth interjected.

'What does "elected" mean?'

Elizabeth explained about votes and ballot papers.

'Does that mean Daddy is famous?' asked Lucy, aged six and one third.

'A little bit.'

* * *

As he had promised, Thompson opened an office in the constituency, in a 1960s shopping mall close to the city centre. It had once hummed with life, but now consisted mainly of struggling coffee shops, a branch of Poundland, a betting shop and an Oxfam bookshop. He tried to make his office as cheerful as possible. It was painted in bright colours with his name – FRED THOMPSON MP – plastered across the entire shopfront in white lettering on a red background above the plate glass window. Posters advertised the local theatre, the food bank, times of surgeries and names and contact details for local councillors. He employed two people, Janice Jeffries, a South Yorkshirewoman of a certain age, whose husband, father and grandfather had worked in Sheffield's now defunct steel mills, and Tom Picton, a bright young graduate fresh out of Hull University whose father was a prominent councillor.

There were two ground-floor rooms. The front office where the staff worked served as a reception. A framed portrait of Harry Perkins had pride of place on the wall facing the door. The spartan rear room, furnished with a desk and half a dozen chairs and decorated at one end with a trade union banner, was where Thompson held his surgeries. The desk was clear apart from a photograph of the children, a few sheets of House of Commons notepaper, a mug containing an assortment of pens and 'in' and 'out' trays. Both empty. Mrs Jeffries liked it that way.

Every MP's surgery has its regulars who stand out among the housing, benefit and immigration cases: the woman who thinks her next-door neighbour is spying on her with an X-ray machine that can see through her wall; the failed asylum seeker; the hopeless litigant, clutching plastic bags full of yellowing documents dating back decades. They have already approached every conceivable authority, including your predecessor, without result and now your turn has come. Disappointment is inevitable; the only decision for the hapless elected representative is how quickly he or she wants to be added to the long list of people who have let them down. Within three months of election, Thompson had been visited by examples of all three stereotypes and many others.

Among his early petitioners was a gaunt, shaven-headed, heavily tattooed man aged about forty who reckoned he was owed a little pot of public money in recompense for what he considered to be a grievous wrong that had been done to him in years gone by. 'I have worked all my life.' He spoke with the vehemence of one who believed that a few years' payment of National Insurance entitled him to live the rest of his life at public expense.

'When did you say you stopped work?'

'Nine years ago. Sacked. Through no fault of my own.'

'What happened?'

'Punched the foreman, but I was provoked.'

'And you haven't worked since?'

'No.'

'So you worked from leaving school until you were aged ...?

'Thirty-two.' His demeanour was surly.

'And you have no plans to work again?'

'How can I? I told you, I'm disabled.'

He looked fit enough, if somewhat battered. His nose had once been broken, there was a lengthy scar on his left cheek and his lower jaw didn't quite align with the upper part of his mouth. It turned out that he had been the victim of a severe beating by three local criminals wielding baseball bats in revenge for some unspecified offence. No arrests had resulted, though the culprits, he claimed, were well known to the police. The incident, he believed, entitled him to a large payment from the Criminal Injuries Compensation Authority.

Thompson solemnly noted the details and promised to look into the matter. The man slowly rose and limped towards the door, turning at the last moment. 'I hope you are not one of those traitors who are plotting to take us back into the EU.' And without waiting for an answer, he was gone, his parting words hanging in the air.

'That man gives me the creeps,' said Mrs Jeffries.

'Me too,' said Thompson. 'I suspect we are destined to see a lot more of him.'

How right he was.

***

A message on a pink slip. 'Call the chief whip's office.' He called and an appointment was arranged for later that evening.

The chief whip, a teacher by profession, was a decent old Scotsman, thought by some of the upwardly mobile to lack the guile and low cunning that his office required.

'A word of advice, son.'

He paused, glancing at the portrait of Keir Hardie that adorned his wall.

'You need to get out from under Harry's shadow. Things have changed a bit since Harry's day. This place is now full of ambitious young thirty-somethings, adept at tweeting and slogan chanting, who think that history began with New Labour. They don't regard the past as a golden age. On the contrary, many of them blame Harry for putting us out of office for the best part of twenty years. Personally, I loved the man, though he might have handled things a little differently.'

'He took on some mighty vested interests.'

'Aye, that he did. But the problem was that he bit off more than he could chew. More than any of us could.'

'Come off it, Bill. He was betrayed by people who were supposed to be on our side. Reg Smith, Lawrence Wainwright ... You know that as well as I do.'

'Maybe, but—'

'We don't yet know the half of it—'

'Listen, son, I'm just offering you some advice. Up to you, but if you wish to achieve anything in this place, don't waste time re-fighting the battles of the past. That's all I'm saying.'

'I appreciate that.'

'Also, you need to remember that, in addition to the young thrusters, there is a bedrock of old codgers who've been sitting around the tea room for twenty years without ever registering the merest ripple on the national consciousness. Salt of the earth, some of them, but they aren't going to take kindly to being leapfrogged by some upstart who has only been here five minutes. Be nice to them. Surprise them. Show them that you haven't got horns coming out of your head.'

'So, what do you advise?'

'Find an issue. Something that resonates with your constituents. Compensation for industrial diseases, something like that. Get some good solid work under your belt, then you can take up something more esoteric. Play your cards right and I'll see if I can smuggle you onto a decent select committee.'

* * *

Later, in the library corridor. 'Ah, Thompson,' boomed the voice of one born to rule. Rupert Farquar, a Tory baronet, a good six feet in height and of considerable girth, who traced his ancestry back to the Normans and who, more to the point, was said to be distantly related to Sir Peregrine Craddock's wife. 'Good to see you here. This place needs a bit of shaking up.'

A firm handshake and then, *sotto voce*, 'Very sorry about what happened to Harry. Bad business. Personally I admired him, though we didn't agree about much.'

'Perhaps we could talk about that some time.'

'Delighted, dear boy. A quiet drink perhaps. Must be a bit discreet though, you don't want to damage a promising career by being seen talking to the likes of me.' He disappeared down the corridor, chuckling.

* * *

Much later, in the members' tea room. 'Looks like we're going to be here half the night. The Tories are fighting to preserve zero-hours contracts. It's moments like this when you realise that, despite what our beloved electorate believe, the gulf between the main parties is really quite large. Nothing motivates Tory backwoodsmen so much as the preservation of bit of social injustice. It was the same with the minimum wage. They used to go around alleging that it would increase unemployment, as if they cared. In the event unemployment went down and nowadays you can't find anyone who is against it. Welcome, by the way. My name is Stephen Carter.'

'Fred Thompson.' They shook hands.

'Yes, I know who you are . . . You're famous round here.'

'Or notorious.'

Carter laughed. 'Depends how you look at it. So far as I'm concerned, anyone who was a friend of Harry's is a friend of mine.'

A commotion at the far end of the room where a Brylcreemed spiv was loudly berating one of the young serving women, a West Indian.

'I *said* I wanted two slices of toast, not one. Don't you understand English?'

The young woman, flustered, was apologising.

'And this tea is as weak as rat's piss. Take it away.'

'I am sorry sir . . .'

'Who on earth's that?'

'That,' whispered Carter, 'is Michael Flather. One of the nastiest pieces of work in this place. Sooner or later he'll come a cropper. Can't come soon enough as far as I'm concerned.'

* * *

It was reported from Tokyo that a half a dozen soldiers of the People's Liberation Army had been captured trying to plant a Chinese flag on a rocky outcrop, off the coast of one of the Diayou islands.

Four

There are certain essential ingredients to a maiden speech. A new member must say something nice about his predecessor and about his constituency. He or she is also advised to avoid controversy, in return for which they can expect to be heard respectfully. Fred Thompson's speech ticked the first two boxes, but not the third, and as a result he encountered a certain amount of good-natured ribbing, but no particular hostility. Generally the speech was accounted a success and congratulations duly flowed. In the absence of approbation from the world outside, Britain's unloved legislators tend to spend an inordinate amount of time congratulating each other on minor triumphs.

It was always inevitable that Fred Thompson would be noticed. As soon as his name appeared on the monitor, members trickled in from the bars and lobbies. Curiously, there seemed more interest from the government benches than from his opposition colleagues. He chose to highlight three issues. The growing divide between the unfortunate and the prosperous; the need to avoid being dragged into a war with China; and what he asserted was the need to stem the flow of economic migrants before, as he put it, 'the sheer weight of numbers collapsed Europe's fragile social systems'. It was this last that attracted most attention, not all of it friendly. 'Scaremongering,' according to one old left-winger. 'Harry would be turning in his grave,' said another. More astute commentators, however, remarked that this was a young man destined to go far. He had demonstrated from the outset that, contrary to what some alleged, he was not after all destined to dwell for ever in the shadow of his old friend and mentor. 'A speech of remarkable maturity,' *The Times* called it.

* * *

They drove north in the brand new Nissan hatchback that had replaced their battered Volvo estate. The children, strapped in the back, were playing I-spy.

'I spy Sherwood Forest, where Robin Hood used to live,' said Fred, pointing at a thicket of oak trees.

'Who was Robin Hood?' asked Lucy.

'A thief,' said Elizabeth, 'but a good one.'

'Why was he a good one?'

'Because he stole from the rich to give to the poor.'

'We've got the DVD,' said Catherine.

'How long ago did Robin Hood live here?' enquired Lucy.

'A long time ago.'

'Before you and Dad were born?'

'Yes.'

'Before Granny and Grandpa?'

'Long before.'

A pause while the little brain whirred.

'If Robin Hood were alive today, would he give us money?'

Before Elizabeth could answer, Catherine chipped in. 'No, he'd take our money and give it to the poor.'

Lucy's face lit up. 'I bet Robin Hood was a member of the Labour Party.'

* * *

They didn't quite move to Sheffield. Instead they rented an apartment in the old mill at Edale, just below Kinder Scout. It wasn't until they'd been there a month that they discovered this was where Perkins' mistress, Molly Spence, had once lived. 'Small world,' said Fred. 'Fate,' said Elizabeth. 'Will it bring us good luck, or bad?'

Every hour or so the little train, running between

Sheffield and Manchester, rattled through the valley. They fell asleep to the soothing sound of water running down the hill behind the house and into what was once the mill stream. The arrangement was supposed to be temporary, but gradually became permanent. No one in the constituency seemed to mind that their MP had not quite fulfilled his promise. Edale was close enough for most people. During the week, when parliament was in session, Fred lodged with old friends in Kennington. Elizabeth remained at home with the children, who quickly made new friends and soon forgot the lovely place in which they had once lived.

* * *

'We have set up a little dining club,' said Jock Steeples, late one evening in an almost deserted members' tea room.

'Who's "we"?'

'Just a few of us, like-minded folk. Assuming, of course, that we still are of like mind.' This last point a reference to those parts of Thompson's maiden speech that had gone down uncomfortably well with the right-wing media.

'Won't it get us into trouble?'

'Not if we're discreet, like. No rules. No programme. Just a few friends, chewing over the issues of the day. A social occasion.' There was a twinkle in his eye. 'Anyway, we don't have to meet on the premises. This place is dead at night since so-called family-friendly hours were introduced – not that most of us can go home to our families. They live too far away.'

'Has it got a name?'

'As a matter of fact it has. We call it "The Friends of Harry Perkins."'

* * *

They met in the upper room of a little club on the fringes of Soho. It was run by an Austrian of Jewish ancestry, whose father had escaped to London just before the *Anschluss*. The walls were hung with pictures of his heroes, an incongruous bunch ranging from Marx and Engels to George Orwell, Mikhail Gorbachev and Pope John Paul II. Also, pen and ink cartoons of George Bernard Shaw, Nye Bevan, Michael Foot and Tony Benn, all apparently one-time visitors to this establishment. Pride of place was reserved for a beaming photograph of Harry Perkins standing with his arm around the proud patron. The dedication read, 'To Otto, one of the best, Harry'.

Besides Jock Steeples, Mrs Cook and Fred Thompson, there were half a dozen others: Stephen Carter, recently encountered in the members' tea room; Jim Evans, the fiery Welshman who had been Perkins' defence secretary, still going strong in his late seventies; Tom Newsome, one-time foreign secretary, whose political career had come to an abrupt end after he had been found in bed with a young woman from Hampstead Labour party; Sir Matt Someone, an elegant, sixtyish man, whose surname he didn't catch, and was said to be a retired civil servant; Anne-Marie Freeman, an occasional *Times* columnist, said to command a large following in the Twittersphere.

Finally, there was a fifty-something woman, whom Thompson didn't immediately recognise. 'Fred, meet Molly who works for a bank in the City.' Steeples put a finger to his lips. 'Shhh. Top secret. She'd be in trouble if she were caught mixing with the likes of us.' The woman smiled sheepishly as she shook hands. She had deep brown eyes, a complexion that suggested she had once lived in a hot climate and, Thompson noted, wore no wedding ring. Her face was familiar. It was a while before the penny dropped. Ah yes, Molly Spence. They hadn't actually met, but she had been briefly famous as the woman whose affair with Harry Perkins had been used to bring him down. What was she doing here?

Jock Steeples, seated at the head of the table, was in charge. He tapped his wine glass. 'Order, order. First, we have to welcome two new members: Fred Thompson, known to most of you, and Molly Spence, who is Something in the City.' Molly was still an attractive woman: blond hair with just a streak of grey, dimpled cheeks and a radiant smile. 'We come from different walks of life, but we have one thing in common. Most of us were friends and admirers of the late Harry Perkins and we all abhor the way in which he was done down.'

'What do we say, if anybody asks what we're up to?' asked Sir Matt Someone who, it transpired, had once, before achieving his present eminence, been a junior official in Perkins' private office. He added, smiling, 'As we say in government, we need a line to take.'

'The line, which has the merit of being true, is that we are just a group of like-minded friends come together for occasional dinners and to mourn our losses, nothing more. Discretion is the order of day. We've been meeting for several months without anybody noticing, but no doubt we will be rumbled sooner or later. We'll cross that bridge when we come to it. In the meantime the rules are clear. What's said in this room stays here. No tweeting, no blogging and, above all, no blabbing.'

* * *

They fell to talking about the latest of Labour's successive election defeats. 'The Labour Party has lost its soul,' remarked Jim Evans. 'All very well to talk about sticking to the centre ground, but the centre ground has moved so far right that it's no longer worth occupying.'

'I sometimes think our historic mission is over,' said Mrs Cook gloomily. 'And that maybe all we can look forward to is another long period of one-party rule until one day another party breaks through. In the meantime all we can do is try to mitigate the worst excesses of the current management.'

'And who might that other party be?' enquired Jock Steeples in a tone that reeked of incredulity. 'The Liberal Democrats have been smashed out of sight. The Scots Nats are away on a trip of their own. The only threat to the Tories comes from the right.'

'Who knows, the Tories may split,' said Stephen Carter.

'Don't bank on it, son. Unlike our lot, the Tories are serious about power. True, they went through a bad patch over Europe, but that's settled now.'

'Or maybe they'll be brought down by a sudden crisis – the collapse of sterling, another banking scandal . . .'

'The bankers can hardly believe their luck,' said Molly quietly. 'They can't believe they got away with it. You should hear them chortling. It's as though the crash never happened.'

Otto the Patron appeared, notebook in hand, to take orders. He had a thick crop of white hair and large eyebrows. They toasted his health. When he had gone the conversation turned to the latest vacancy for a Labour leader.

'Remind me. How many leaders have we got through since Harry?' enquired Mrs Cook.

'Four ... no, five,' said Jim Evans.

'Aye,' said Tom Newsome, 'and none of them any use. We're further away from power now than at any time in the last forty years.'

'How about the current crop of candidates?' asked Sir Matt. 'Who do you favour?'

'None of the above,' said Newsome. 'Second-raters every one. Too bland, too apologetic, too managerial. We need someone with a bit of passion and personality, not a desiccated calculating machine.'

'But who at the same time doesn't frighten Middle England,' added Carter.

'Maybe young Fred here is the answer to our prayers,' said Steeples amid laughter.

FIVE

A statement from the Pentagon announced that the US Pacific Fleet was three days' sailing from Japanese waters. In Tokyo, the captured Chinese soldiers were paraded on television prompting further outrage in Beijing. In New York the UN Secretary-General summoned an emergency meeting of the Security Council which broke up amid much shouting and table banging. The secretary general's offer to mediate fell upon deaf ears.

In the House of Commons the foreign secretary made a statement. As usual with such pronouncements, it was a near-perfect replica of one issued by the US State Department two hours earlier. The situation, said the foreign secretary, was grave. The world was closer to war than at any time since the Cuban missile crisis. He urged restraint on all sides and added that Britain would be sending a frigate to join the American flotilla. This was followed by a big bout of me-too-ism as senior members on all sides vied to demonstrate their grasp of matters international and diplomatic, but no one had anything useful to suggest.

'In the good old days,' remarked Rupert Farquar afterwards in the tea room, 'we'd have sent a gunboat.'

'Isn't that what we are doing?' said Thompson.

'Ah yes, but in those days we wouldn't have been tagging along behind the Americans. One British gunboat would have been enough to keep the natives in their place.' There was a wide grin across his ample features. You could never tell when Farquar was being serious or not. Anyway, he added, everything would all calm down in a few days.

'Until the next time. The Chinese have a long list of demands – disputes with just about all their neighbours.'

'But they have always been cautious about pursuing them. War isn't in their interests any more than it is in ours. They've too much to lose.'

'Let's hope so.'

'Amen to that,' said Farquar. And then, suddenly lowering his voice. 'On another matter. Got a chap who wants to meet you. Might learn something to your advantage.' He glanced around to make sure no one was listening. 'Very hush-hush. Need to be discreet. Come to my house after the vote tomorrow and all will be revealed.'

* * *

As Thompson had predicted, the angry, tattooed white male was a regular visitor to his surgeries. Within a week he was back, demanding to know whether a reply had been received from the Criminal Injuries Compensation Authority. His name was Thomas Walter Merton and it turned out he had a lengthy criminal record, mainly for crimes of violence. As the weeks passed, his tone became more menacing. 'Don't think you can fob me off,' he snarled. 'I'll keep chasing you until this is sorted. I'll never give up.'

In due course a reply was received, but the news was not good.

'It says here that you have criminal convictions for violence . . .' said Thompson quietly.

'So what? That's got nothing to do with this.'

' . . . It says you served a prison sentence for beating up a woman. Is that true?'

'She's a lying bitch, it was a miscarriage of justice.'

'The point is, Mr Merton, that the Authority will not entertain claims from anyone with a conviction for violence.'

A moment's silence. And then, without warning, Merton leaned forward and slammed his fist down on the desk that separated them. The photo of Lucy and Catherine crashed to the floor, glass shattering. Mrs Jeffries let out a low cry. 'Now look here . . .' said Thompson weakly.

'No, you look here . . .' bawled Merton, eyes bulging, his face crimson with rage. 'It's your job to sort this out and, if you don't, I'll sort you out.'

'Don't you threaten me.' Thompson had recovered his composure.

'Just you try me.' And with that Merton stormed out.

'Phew,' said Mrs Jeffries, 'I thought he was going to brain you. Did you notice, by the way, he has a Union Jack tattooed on his right arm?'

* * *

The London residence of the Farquars was a street of Queen Anne houses, a stone's throw from the Palace of Westminster. The light was fading when Fred arrived. Farquar himself, resplendent in a maroon velvet smoking jacket, answered the door.

'Ah, Thompson. Do come in. My friend is upstairs. A quiet word before we go up. Not a word to anyone about my role in this – or his. You can use his information as you see fit, but it's not to be attributed. Understand?'

'Absolutely.'

'Good man. Knew I could count on you.' Farquar patted

his shoulder and ushered Thompson up the stairs, the wall lined with *Vanity Fair* cartoons of nineteenth-century statesmen, to a panelled drawing room on the first floor. On either side of the fireplace, watercolours. 'By Nick Ridley,' said Farquar. 'Remember him? One of the geniuses who gave us the poll tax. A talented painter, though.'

Above the mantelpiece, illuminated by an overhead light, an oil of sunflowers. 'Is that what I think it is?'

'It is indeed. My grandfather came across it in a flea market in France in the twenties. Had an eye for a bargain and that certainly was a bargain. Worth more than the house.'

A man was standing by the window, puffing a cigarette. Aged about fifty. Small, bald, agitated. Out of place in a Queen Anne drawing room. 'And this is Mr ... Well you don't need to know his name. Let's just say he is a constituent of mine.' Farquar addressed the man, 'This is Mr Frederick Thompson.' The last person to call Fred by his full first name was a long-dead and much-feared aunt.

The man offered a weak handshake. Farquar poured two generous whiskies and handed one to Thompson. 'Do sit down, gentlemen.'

They sat. The little man perched bolt upright, precariously on the edge of the sofa

'Mr ... is it all right if I call you William for purposes of identification?' The man nodded weakly. Farquar began again, 'William here has come to me with some very interesting information about one of our colleagues. Perhaps I should say one of *my* colleagues.'

'Who?'

'A name that will be well known to you: Michael Christopher Flather.'

'The one who is always going on about immigrants?'

'The very same. Tabloid hero. Rising star. A future leader, some say. Heaven forbid.' Only last week Flather had been making headlines for leading a noisy demonstration of righteous Home Counties citizens to the site of a proposed migrant hostel. 'Any idea how he made his money?'

'Tell me.'

'Haulage. Made a fortune shipping live calves to the Continent. Disgusting trade. Did my best to get it banned, but to no avail. EU rules and all that. Eventually he sold the company for squillions. What's interesting though is not what he was taking out of the country, but what he was bringing in. William here used to work for him.' A pause. 'William, Tell Mr Thompson what you have told me.'

'You will keep my name out of it, won't you, sir?'

'You have my word.'

'Well, of course, Mr Flather's respectable now. But it

wasn't always that way. Self-made, you see. Began with just one vehicle which he drove himself. By the finish he had several hundred. Started with him as a driver, I did, but then I went into the office. That was where I found out about it.'

'About what?'

'There were two businesses. One that was legit and one that wasn't. Two sets of books. One that was declared to the revenue and one that wasn't.'

'And what was he bringing in?'

'That's just it. That business last week was the final straw. I saw him on the television news outside that hostel and I thought "you cheeky bugger."'

He paused. A sliver of a smile crossed his lips. 'He was bringing in migrants. Illegal migrants.'

Farquar looked at Fred, beaming. 'Couldn't make it up, could you?'

'You can prove this?' said Fred sceptically.

'Well, sir, I can only tell you what I saw.' The man was warming to his theme now, speaking with confidence. 'It was a while ago. Long before everything started falling apart in Syria and the like. Actually immigration wasn't much of an issue then. Nothing about it in the papers. One night I had to work late and a lorry arrived back from France. It had been to Brindisi in southern Italy, where the cattle are off-loaded for the Middle East.'

'And?'

'A lot of men got out. Dark skinned. I heard later they were from Albania.'

'And what happened?'

'Shortly after, a minibus arrived and they were taken away. I don't know where to.'

'How do you know it wasn't just a bit of private enterprise on the part of the driver?'

'Because I asked about it – discreet, like – the next day. There was man in the office, Stanley something or other, a cockney geezer. He didn't have much to do with the rest of us, but was always in and out of Mr Flather's office. Very hush-hush. I waited until he and I were alone and then said, sort of casual like, "Who were all them blokes I saw in the yard last night?" At first he came over ignorant. "What blokes? I don't know nothing about no blokes." Later, as I was getting ready to leave, he came up to me real close and whispered that if I knew what was good for me, I'd keep my mouth shut. It was nobody's business, except him and the boss.'

'And that was that, was it?'

'No, no, it wasn't. I let it go at the time, but it kept nagging at me. And then one day, about a year later. I came across the lorry driver. In Lanzarote, of all places. I was there with my missus. He was there with his. Recognised him at once on account of the dragon tattooed on his arm. Albert his name was. By this time he'd moved on. Had a bit of a falling out with the boss, I heard. By now he was working for one of them big supermarket chains. We had a chat about one thing and another and then I said, out of the blue, "Who were all those foreign-looking blokes I saw getting out of the back of your lorry a year gone May?" Went pale, he did. Then he looked across to make sure his missus was out of earshot and said, very quietly, "Albanians. We was smuggling Albanians. Only Stanley in the office knew about it and four or five of us drivers. Sworn to secrecy, we were. And paid to keep our mouths shut. Easy then, it was. Not like today when they're running infrared scanners over every lorry."'

Thompson sipped his whisky. 'That doesn't prove that Mr Flather knew about it.'

'That's what I said, but Albert said, "'Course he did – a couple of times he was there when Stanley paid off the drivers. Once he was even there when the Albanians were being offloaded."'

'What happened to this Stanley?'

'Last I heard he'd retired, to a condo in Florida. Did very nicely out of it, so I'm told. I left soon after the business was sold and the new owners tried to put us all on zero-hours contracts. Got my own business now. A little newsagent's.'

'Who else knew what was going on?' said Farquar.

'Well there was a woman in the office. Mr Flather's personal secretary. I don't think she was in on it, but she must have noticed. Her name was Eames, Rosalind Eames. In her fifties. Probably retired now.'

'Could you find her?'

'Maybe. We've a couple of friends in common. You will keep my name out of this, won't you?'

'I can assure you we will,' said Farquar gravely. 'You have been most helpful, Mr . . . er, William. Most helpful.' They stood and shook hands and Farquar showed the little man out, gesturing to Thompson that he should stay put. They disappeared down the stairs, the little man protesting that he just wanted a quiet life and that he would never have got involved, but he was sick and tired of hearing Flather ranting about immigrants. Farquar assuring him that he had done right. 'I'm not that keen on foreigners myself,' the little man was heard to say as the front door closed, 'but I can't stand all that hype-ocrisy.'

* * *

A minute later and Farquar was back in the drawing room, refilling their glasses. 'Well, dear boy, what did you make of that?'

'Fascinating, but why are you letting me in on this? Why not just tip off your friends in high places and let them do the necessary?'

He leaned forward, a wicked grin illuminating his plump visage. 'Because, dear boy, I want you to bring the bastard down.' A pause and then he continued. 'If I tip off the higher-ups, it will all be hushed up. A quiet word and Flather will announce that he is standing down for family reasons and disappear back into the cesspit from which he crawled. I want him *eviscerated*.' There was a malicious gleam in Farquar's eye. He went on, 'You need to understand that I am one of an almost extinct breed in my party – a one-nation Tory. I loathe these greedy, prof-iteering, tax-avoiding pinstripes who grew up believing the Thatcher decade was a golden age. And Flather is one of the worst.

'Plus,' he added quietly, 'we need a bit of detective work, and you are just the man for that.'

* * *

A statement from the foreign ministry in Tokyo announced that, as a gesture of conciliation and in the interests of world peace, the captured Chinese soldiers would be repatriated. Meanwhile there were unconfirmed reports, in an obscure scientific journal, that Japan had for the last twenty years been secretly developing nuclear weapons. A spokesman for the Japanese foreign ministry denounced the suggestion as an outrageous slur, but didn't quite get round to a categorical denial.

Six

In death Harry Perkins acquired more friends than he had ever had in life. A bronze bust was unveiled in the members' lobby, on a ledge just to the left of Clement Attlee, another of Perkins' heroes. Madam Speaker presided in a lobby jam-packed with the great and good of the political class. The new Labour leader, Sylvia Jones, a bland, pleasant woman who radiated mediocrity, made a gracious little speech, the gist of which was that although she and Harry had their differences, no one could be happier than she that Perkins was taking his rightful place among the giants of British politics. 'May God look sideways on you,' muttered Jock Steeples audibly enough to cause heads to turn and even a fit of giggles among several of those closest.

As they were filing out into the library corridor, the vast shadow of Farquar loomed. 'Ah, there you are, Thompson.

I've got something for you.' He took a small envelope from his pocket and slid it into Thompson's hand. 'Let me know how you get on,' he whispered. And with that he was gone, disappearing in the direction of what was once the smoking room.

* * *

'Who did you say you are?' She peered at him over the top of horn-rimmed glasses. An elegant, though fading woman, whose demeanour radiated disappointment. No sign of a wedding ring.

Thompson took out his House of Commons pass and handed it to her. She examined it carefully and returned it to him. She was harvesting sweet peas on a trellis attached to the garden wall.

'I want to talk to you about Michael Flather.'

'Michael who?' She affected not to recognise the name.

'You used to work for him.'

'Oh, him.' Her tone suggested that he was someone about whom she did not wish to be reminded. 'You'd better come in.'

She led him to the back door. It was an ordinary house on the edge of a quaint West Sussex village. One of half a dozen former council properties that had long since been sold off, a leftover from the days when local authorities took responsibility for housing those who could not afford a home of their own.

'You live here alone?' asked Thompson for want of something to say.

'Yes, since my mother died.' She indicated a photograph of an elderly lady on the dresser.

She made two mugs of mint tea. They sat at the kitchen table. 'Does Mr Flather know you are here?'

'No. Nobody does.'

'Good.'

'When did you last see him?'

'Ten, maybe twelve years ago.'

'And how long did you work for him?'

'Five years. I left when the business changed hands.'

'Did you like him?'

'Does that matter?'

A large ginger cat strolled in, took one look at Thompson and did an immediate about-turn. 'He doesn't like strangers,' she said.

'What were your responsibilities?'

'I was his personal assistant. I looked after his appointments diary, correspondence and kept the books.'

'I understand there were two sets of books.'

Silence.

'The ones I am in interested were kept by a man called Stanley.'

Her eyes didn't quite meet his. 'I wouldn't know about that,' she said quietly.

'I think you do.'

'Why don't you ask Stanley?'

'I would if I knew where he was to be found.'

'He went abroad. America, I think.'

'So I understand. I take it you don't have an address for him?'

'No.'

'In that case I must rely on you. What were Stanley's responsibilities?'

She hesitated. 'I . . . I . . .' The ginger cat reappeared and, steering a wide circle around Thompson, made its way to a cushion by the boiler. 'He ran the other part of the business. I was never involved with that. The accounts, all the paperwork were separate. Stan dealt directly with Mr Flather. He was very discreet.'

'What was the other part of the business?

'I . . . I don't know.'

'I think you do.'

'I am sorry, I can't help you.'

'It was people smuggling, wasn't it?'

She didn't get indignant, denying all, rushing to her former employer's defence. There was no 'how dare you'.

No demand that he produce evidence or withdraw the outrageous slur. She just repeated quietly, 'I can't help you.' All the while looking at the table.

He pressed her for several minutes, but she was adamant. So far as she was aware it was a haulage business. Nothing more, nothing less. Never once did she raise her voice. On the contrary, the more he pressed the quieter her replies became until they were almost inaudible.

* * *

He got up to leave. She walked behind him to the door and then to the garden gate. At the gate he hesitated and turned towards her. 'Mrs ... Eames ...'

'I am not married.'

'Ms Eames, this is not the end of the matter. There will be an inquiry. Maybe prosecutions in due course. Your name is in the frame. Unless you help me, your next visitor may well be a police officer.'

She turned pale. Looked at the ground, fidgeted, sighed deeply. At length she said, 'You had better come back inside.'

They returned to the kitchen. The sweet peas were in a basket on the table.

'If I help, will you promise to keep my name out of it?'

'I'll do my best, but I can offer no guarantee. You may have to make a statement.'

She gave a deep sigh. 'I knew that, sooner or later, someone would come. As soon as I saw him on the television going on about migrants, I thought, "You are living dangerously." Reckless, that's what he was. Everything he did involved risk – and greed. He didn't give a fig about anyone but himself. He was a class A shit.'

She spoke with such passion that it occurred to Thompson there was more to her relationship with Michael Flather than met the eye. 'How well did you know him?'

She took a deep breath. 'If you must know, we had an affair. It lasted three years, and then, when I was no longer of any use to him, he dumped me. The biggest mistake of my life.'

'Tell me about the other side of the business. The one that Stan ran.'

'As you say, it was a people-smuggling operation. Cattle were being trucked to southern Italy. The trucks were then hosed down and filled with people. Well, not filled. Actually just a handful at a time. There were false ceilings, compartments in the roof in which they had to hide before they crossed frontiers. Albanians mostly, but there were others. Some from the Middle East. They paid big money.'

'When did you find out what was going on?'

'Michael told me. He needed my help. The money had been going into someone else's bank account, not his. But whoever it was got cold feet and backed out. He needed someone he trusted to open another account and, like a mug, I agreed.'

* * *

'Well, my boy,' said Jock Steeples. 'You've hit the jackpot.' They were seated at the far end of the House of Commons terrace, beyond the sign that said 'Members Only'. The seats around them were empty.

'The question is, how do we handle it? First, you need to be sure of your facts.'

'I have a statement from his former personal assistant – and mistress – signed and witnessed by a solicitor.'

'And?'

'Well, there's the man who first alerted me. He also used to work for Flather, but he's not going to stick his head above the parapet. Also, there's a lorry driver called Albert, but I haven't spoken to him.'

'I think you should,' said Steeples. 'You need two sources for something as explosive as this – that's what I was taught when I was a young journalist.'

* * *

Albert, the driver, was easily traced. Farquar merely went back to William who gave him a surname and pointed him in the direction of a council estate in Croydon, all the while insisting that he wanted his name kept out of it. Armed with that information, all that was required was a trawl of the electoral register.

It was a 1950s estate, from the golden age of public housing. Three-up, two-down houses, each with a little garden front and back. The sort of place that had once been entirely white working class, solid Labour until Mrs Thatcher had started selling off council houses at knock-down prices. Most of the houses had been bought; you could tell which ones by the new porches, Velux windows in the roof, brightly coloured front doors. Even a solar panel or two. Many were now in the hands of buy-to-let landlords. Most of these were instantly identifiable, too, by their unkempt gardens and overflowing rubbish bins. Albert's front garden, in contrast, was neat and trim, a rose spilled over the porch, catmint lined the path to the front door.

Albert's missus answered. The television was on in the background. 'Albert, there's someone to see you. Says he's a member of parliament.' In the old days a visit from an MP would have been a big deal, but the age of deference had long since passed.

Albert appeared, dressed in overalls. He hadn't been home long. A big man, overweight, nicotine-stained fingers. Mrs Albert was a mouse by comparison. He peered at Thompson from the gloom of the hallway. 'An MP? What does he want with me? You're wasting your time round here, mate. I haven't voted for twenty years. Not since that Tony Blair let in all those migrants. All over the place, they are. We've got hundreds of them round here.'

'Actually, migrants – that's exactly what I want to talk to you about. Can I come in?'

Hesitantly, Mrs Albert stood aside. Thompson stepped gingerly into the hallway and followed Albert into the sitting room. A copy of the *Daily Express*, open at the racing page, lay on the sofa. Albert plonked himself in an armchair by the television. Fred sat down opposite him without waiting to be asked. *EastEnders* was on the telly, a lot of unhappy people shouting at each other. 'Would you mind turning that off?'

Slowly, with a little show of reluctance, Albert leaned over and switched off the television. The tattoo on his biceps was of a dragon breathing fire.

'What did you say your name was?'

'Thompson, Fred Thompson.' He proffered his MP's photo pass. Albert examined it carefully and handed it back.

'Never heard of you.'

'I've not been in parliament that long.'

'What can I do for you?'

Mrs Albert, hovering in the doorway, asked if he wanted a cup of tea. An offer Thompson gratefully accepted, if only to break the ice.

'You used to work for Michael Flather, the Tory MP.'

'That was years ago. What of it?'

'Mr Flather takes a strong line on immigrants, doesn't he?'

'What's that got to do with me?' His tone was quieter, now. Cautious, even. Somewhere in the far distance a little light was coming on.

'But it wasn't always so, was it?'

'What do you mean?'

'What was it you did for Mr Flather?'

'I drove trucks. Haulage, that was the business.'

'And what did those trucks carry?'

'All sorts. Goods, cattle . . .'

'People . . .?'

'I don't know nothing about that. I think it's time you was going.'

At which point Mrs Albert reappeared with two mugs of tea and a plate of chocolate biscuits. Thompson ate one, munching slowly. 'Are those your grandchildren?' he enquired, indicating photos of three small cherubs on the mantelpiece.

Albert glowered; Mrs Albert glowed. 'Jordan, the youngest. He's four. And that's his sister, Chelsea, aged five. Belong to my oldest boy Alan, they do. My other boy, Harry,' she indicated a photo of a muscular young man in his late twenties, 'has one and another one is on the way. That's his, Maggie. Cheeky little monkey, she is.' She handed the photo to Thompson who made a little show of admiring it and handed it back.

'Have you got children, Mr Thompson?'

'Two – girls aged six and eight.'

'Lovely. I wish I'd had a girl. Not that I am unhappy with my boys,' she added hastily. 'Turned out well, they have. Alan works for Honda in Swindon and Harry's a chef at a hotel in the Midlands. I wish we saw more of them, but they're always busy, what with one thing and another.'

'I think you'd better leave us alone, Mother,' said Albert firmly. 'Mr Thompson and I have some important business to discuss.' Mrs Albert promptly disappeared.

'Now, where were we?' said Albert. A hint of menace in his voice.

'We were discussing Michael Flather. Or rather his business. He was smuggling migrants, wasn't he?'

'I wouldn't know nothing about that.' Even so, he did not sound shocked at the suggestion.

'Oh I think you would.'

'And what makes you think that . . .?'

'Because you were up to your neck in it.'

There was a long silence. Outside two youths were kicking a football against a wall. Thud, thud, thud.

'Who told you that? Tell me and I'll kick his arse . . .'

'It's true, isn't it?'

Another long pause. The football hit the wall – once, twice, three times.

'Fucking hypocrite, he is. It was his idea, not mine.'

'What was?'

'We was delivering cattle to southern Italy and coming back empty. One day he asks me if I want to make some serious money. He knew someone, he said, who was interested in bringing in foreigners. Not many, like. Just a handful at a time. Albanians mainly, but some from further afield – Iranians, one or two Afghans. He had a false compartment fitted, with air vents. They only used it when we reached the Channel. We used to pull up in a forest about ten miles short of Calais, clear up the debris in the back and then they'd disappear into the compartment. Usually I dropped them off in a lay-by outside Dover and someone would pick them up, but on one occasion no one turned up and I had to bring them back to the depot. That's when we got seen. That William who worked in the office. He was working late. I bet it was him that told you, wasn't it? Came across him once in Lanzarote. Nervous little fellow. I should have known he couldn't be trusted to keep his mouth shut.'

'Actually, it was Mrs Eames. Remember her? She worked in the office. Knew all Flather's secrets.'

'You mean that Rosalind? Stuck up so-and-so, she was. Very proper, she appeared, but we always reckoned she was sleeping with Flather.'

Thompson said nothing. The football hit the window.

'Bloody kids,' said Albert, half rising from the armchair. 'So what the hell made her blab?'

'How would I know?' said Thompson innocently, as if he had nothing to do with it. 'She couldn't bear the hypocrisy, I guess.'

'Well, to tell you the truth, neither could I . . .' He paused, perhaps realising it was a bit late to claim the moral high ground. 'What do you want with me?'

'I want you to make a sworn statement, setting out exactly what you know. Mrs Eames has already made one.'

'Oh no. Now look here, Fred, Frederick, or whatever your name is, I don't want no trouble.'

Thompson had the upper hand now. 'Well, Albert – may I call you Albert? – I'm afraid it's too late for that. If you do co-operate though, we can probably keep you out of jail.'

'Jail?' The blood drained from Albert's face. 'It was years ago, I only made half a dozen trips – ten at the most.

In the end I got cold feet and told Mr Flather I was leaving. He wasn't best pleased about that.'

'If this goes to court,' said Thompson doing his best to sound sympathetic, 'your best hope is to give evidence against Flather.'

'I don't know about that. Mr Flather has got some nasty friends.'

'In that case,' said Thompson, 'I'm afraid you'll go down with him.'

* * *

It took a while to get a statement out of Albert. Two more visits, in fact. The first time, he failed to show up to a prearranged appointment at the office of a local solicitor. Second time round Thompson appeared unannounced on his doorstep accompanied by Stephen Carter who, it transpired, was a solicitor by profession. Mrs Albert, looking distinctly uneasy, answered the door. 'He's not in,' she said.

'I think he is,' said Thompson. 'My colleague and I have just watched him park his car, walk down the garden path and let himself in the front door. This is Mr Carter, by the way. He's a lawyer.'

They found Albert in the kitchen, scoffing his dinner. 'No hurry,' said Thompson. 'We've got all evening.' It took nearly two hours, with interruptions, to tap the statement into Thompson's laptop. Albert's memory lapsed at convenient points. Several times they had to go back over old ground as Albert's memory improved. He had difficulty with names and dates, but eventually a coherent narrative emerged. Thompson opened his wheelie bag and took out an Epson printer, printing out first a draft and then two top copies. Reluctantly Albert signed and Carter witnessed. 'What happens next?' asked Albert as he showed them to the door. 'Will it be in the papers?'

'I imagine it might.'

SEVEN

One night, at about two in the morning, Catherine appeared in Fred and Elizabeth's bedroom. Until now she had always been a good sleeper.

'What is it, my sunshine?'

'Daddy, my head hurts.' She was holding a hand to her forehead.

'Here, let me give it a kiss ... Is that better?'

He stroked her blond hair. 'Now go back to bed and sleep tight.'

The little nugget disappeared, but within the hour she was back, still rubbing her forehead, tears welling. Elizabeth gave her an aspirin and she went back to bed, but at breakfast she was still complaining of a sore head.

* * *

'We need a strategy,' said Steeples, when Fred produced the second affidavit. 'You've got to come across as acting responsibly, rather than some left-wing firebrand. As it happens, we're in luck, there's a debate on migration coming up the week after next. Flather's bound to want to contribute. I suggest we pay a visit to the chief whip and tell him what's afoot. You'll also need to inform our front bench team. On the day, but not before, we might tip off a couple of journalists – the *Mail* and the *Guardian*, I suggest. *Mail* readers are his core supporters, they'll roast him.' He licked his lips in anticipation.

'One other thing. You need to give Flather notice that you'll be mentioning his name. No need to go into detail, just enough to ensure his presence. Drop him a note, just before the debate.'

* * *

The day came. Flather was in his usual seat, to the left of the Treasury bench, two rows back, smug, arrogant, righteous, surrounded by smirking acolytes, no idea of what was about to hit him. Thompson took a seat almost exactly opposite. Jock Steeples, Mrs Cook and Stephen Carter were lined up behind him. The debate was on a government motion so the chamber soon filled. The front bench teams were in their place, the opposition chief whip, glancing back at Thompson, giving him a friendly nod.

Thompson's note, marked 'personal and urgent' was delivered by messenger, several minutes into the home secretary's speech. He watched, trembling with anticipation, as it passed along the row. To Thompson's dismay, Flather merely glanced at the envelope and tucked it into an inside pocket. After a minute or two, curiosity got the better of him. He reached into his jacket, extracted the envelope, scowled, examined both sides and opened it. He read it once, twice, three times; a frown creased his forehead. He showed it to his neighbours on either side who shrugged. Then he peered around the chamber, trying to identify the author. Eventually Thompson had to be pointed out to him. For a long thirty seconds Flather, jaw clamped tight, lips curved downwards, simply stared. Thompson gave a wan smile and then broke off eye contact.

The home secretary spoke. Although from the right of her party her tone was moderate, balanced, responsible. Yes, migration was a problem, but the causes were many and complex and, contrary to what some alleged, there were no simple solutions. At the mention of 'simple solutions' Flather rose. At first the home secretary ignored him, but as the cries of 'give way' grew louder, she eventually sat down.

A deathly hush came over the House as Flather rose. 'I am grateful to the home secretary for giving way.' He paused.

'Get on with it,' came a lone voice from the other side.

'Is the home secretary aware – indeed, I am sure she is – that many hardworking British citizens are losing faith in the ability of politicians to cope with the rising tide of migrants who are taking their jobs, their houses and harassing our women ...?'

From the opposition benches and, *sotto voce*, from one or two members on the government side, cries of 'shameful'.

Flather waited for the noise to subside. 'Is she also aware that, if the government will not act, then our long-suffering people will?' He sat down to a bout of vigorous hear-hearing from the acolytes and glum silence from most on the government benches who stared blankly at their order papers.

'Home Secretary,' called the speaker, and she was on her feet again. An elegant, somewhat hard-faced woman with steel in her voice. 'Forced repatriation is *not*, and never will be, the policy of this government and the hon-ourable gentleman and his friends should be aware that anyone who incites or engages in violence towards foreign nationals will feel the full weight of the law.' Her words were drowned by cheers – mostly, it has to be said, from the opposition benches. Flather slouched, smirking, while the little coterie of acolytes seated around him patted his back. He was unbothered by the fact that he had little overt support on his own side. His base lay in blighted council estates, leafy suburbs and on the executive committees of not a few constituency associations.

After the front bench spokesmen had said their piece, numbers thinned. The home secretary departed and the press gallery emptied of all save agency reporters. To Thompson's dismay even Flather disappeared, in the direction of the tea room, no doubt to celebrate his triumph with a mug of tea and a piece of fruit cake. He had got his sound bite for the six o'clock news and that was all that mattered.

An hour passed and then another as the chamber emptied. Media deadlines came and went. Thompson began to despair. 'Don't worry, son,' said Steeples, 'they'll all come streaming back when you get up. The whips have put the word around.'

Eventually, with less than an hour to go before the closing speeches, Thompson was called. The green benches were two thirds empty. 'Mr Deputy Speaker ...' (the speaker had long since departed) 'we have all witnessed the disgraceful, shameful scenes outside migrants' hostels in the coastal towns. We are all aware of the recent spate of attacks on migrants and their families. And all responsible politicians and others in positions of leadership will know that they should do nothing to inflame what is already a very delicate situation.'

As Jock Steeples had predicted, members on all sides, seeing Thompson's name on the monitors, began to trickle back into the chamber. The shadow home secretary took his seat and before long the home secretary herself was in her place, after which the trickle of members into the chamber became a flood. The press gallery was filling up, too. Steeples and Mrs Cook had been busy.

'The home secretary spoke for all of us ... Perhaps I should rephrase that, *almost* all of us,' he glanced across at the empty seats where Flather and his acolytes had been sitting, 'when she replied to the honourable member for Surrey South earlier in the debate.' At the mention of his name Flather, trailed by half a dozen of his followers, miraculously reappeared and took his seat. 'The House should be aware, however, that the member for Surrey South was not always the opponent of uncontrolled immigration that he affects to be today ...' Suddenly Flather was sitting bolt upright.

'Speak slowly,' Steeples had advised. 'Make every word count.' The Commons has a notoriously short attention span, but Thompson had captured the attention of the entire House.

'In a previous incarnation, the honourable gentleman was a haulage contractor, a self-made man ...'

'Madam Speaker . . .' (the speaker, too, was back in her seat, and one of the acolytes was on his feet) 'Madam Speaker, what has this to do with the motion . . .?'

'I am listening carefully. I am sure the honourable gentleman will stick to the subject on the order paper.'

'Rest assured, Madam Speaker, I will. We are talking about migration, *illegal* migration.' Flather had visibly paled. 'As a haulier, the principal part of the honourable gentleman's business involved the transport of live cattle to southern Italy—'

'On a point of order, Madam Speaker.' One of the acolytes was on his feet. 'What has this got to do with migration?'

The speaker, too, was growing impatient. 'I am sure the honourable member is about to make his point.'

'Indeed I am, Madam Speaker. The House should be aware that there was another, darker side to the honourable member's business activities. He was smuggling illegal migrants into the UK.'

Total, stunned, silence.

And then, 'Madam Speaker, this is outrageous.' Flather was on his feet, flailing. 'The honourable gentleman has made a very grave accusation. I hope he has proof of what he is alleging.'

'I do indeed, Madam Speaker.' Thompson brandished his statements. 'These are copies of affidavits sworn by two former employees of the honourable gentleman ...' Thompson struggled to make himself heard above the uproar '... which I will make available to the appropriate authorities.' With that he sat down.

Flather, pale-faced, had slumped in his seat, all the arrogance suddenly knocked out of him. It was left to the acolytes to express indignation on his behalf, bobbing up and down, making bogus points of order to which the speaker gave short shrift. Most of the Tories just sat paralysed.

* * *

Flather was not seen again in the House of Commons. His friends melted away, scarcely able to recall that they had ever known him. He did not respond to requests for interviews. Telephones both at home and at his office went unanswered. There were rumours that he had fled abroad. Upon receipt of the affidavits the chairman of the Standards and Privileges Committee announced an inquiry which was swiftly overtaken by the news that the Metropolitan Police were launching a criminal investigation. Two days later the government chief whip put out a terse statement announcing that Flather was resigning his seat with immediate effect.

* * *

Catherine's headaches grew worse. Elizabeth took her to the doctor who referred her to the hospital for a scan. The news was not good. They were called to a meeting with the oncologist. He did not beat about the bush. 'I am afraid Catherine has a tumour. She will need treatment, urgently.'

Suddenly the world stood still. They could no longer hear the bustle in the corridor outside, the banging of trolleys, the sound of traffic. Besides this everything else was trivial.

'What are her chances?' whispered Elizabeth

'Depends whether or not it is malignant. Most tumours are benign, in which case her chances are good.'

'And if it is not benign?'

'About fifty-fifty.'

Eight

'Congratulations, my boy, you are the hero of the hour,' said Jock Steeples when the Friends assembled for dinner a few days after the event. Otto the Patron was beside himself with joy. *'Wunderbar,'* he said, his rugged face illuminated by a broad smile. 'Bloody, effing *wunderbar.'* A bottle of Pol Roger appeared. 'On the house,' he said, raising a glass to Thompson. He then produced a camera and insisted on their being photographed together. 'I shall want you to sign this. You've earned a place on my wall of fame.'

'If I were you,' advised Steeples when Otto had disappeared, 'I'd say as little as possible. There will be a trial and you may be called upon to give evidence.'

'And don't let it go to your head,' whispered Mrs Cook. 'An inflated ego can be crippling in our line of business.'

'No chance,' replied Thompson mysteriously, 'I have something much more important to worry about.'

'Such as?' said Mrs Cook, but he didn't elaborate and she didn't press him.

* * *

Congratulations flowed in. In the House Thompson couldn't walk five paces without colleagues slapping him on the back. Handwritten notes marked 'personal and private' appeared on the letter board, many from Tory members glad to see the back of Flather. 'Every democracy needs people like you,' read one. 'A great public service,' said another. Letters and postcards arrived by the sack load, emails by the thousand. Many bore messages which began, 'I do not share your politics but . . .' Strangers approached him in the street and on the train. He was the subject of laudatory profiles in the Sunday newspapers. As Steeples advised, however, Thompson kept his head down, affecting an air of modesty. Indeed, some quietly remarked that, for a man who had just scored a great triumph, he looked positively miserable. But then, of course, he knew something they didn't. Not an hour passed without his thinking of Catherine. He tried to tell himself that it would be all right. Tragedies were for other people, not for lucky lives like his. But deep down he feared the worst.

* * *

CHRIS MULLIN

A message from the leader's office. Mrs Jones would like a word. Sylvia Jones was an elegant woman in her late forties. Her husband was something in the City, so money wasn't a problem. She had risen by the classic route: St Hugh's College, Oxford, a year at Harvard, ministerial adviser, MP – the product of an all-woman shortlist while still in her late twenties. A junior member of Harry Perkins' government, she was one of the few bright stars of the long years of opposition which followed. The first female to be elected Labour leader in her own right. No one doubted her ability, or that behind that undoubted charm there was a steely resolve, but somehow it did not make up for the lack of passion. Her views were the product of diligent study rather than life experience, and it showed. Polls suggested that the public had yet to warm to her.

'A long time since our paths last crossed.' She shook his hand warmly.

Indeed. In those days Thompson had been a mover and shaker at the heart of government and she the lowest form of ministerial life, struggling to make a name for herself. How times change.

'This must all seem a bit of a let-down to you,' she said. 'After all, you've been at the heart of power. None of us have.'

'Not at all,' he said, but he knew she was right. It was unlikely that he would ever again taste power, at least nothing like what he had enjoyed in those two glorious years with Harry.

She motioned him to an armchair. 'Well, you've certainly got off to a good start. Not many newcomers make a splash like you have.'

'Actually, I fear I may have done the Tories a service. Without Flather and his mates, they will be respectable again.'

'Yes,' she said archly, 'that point had occurred to me.'

There was an awkward silence. In truth they didn't have a lot in common. At length she said, 'Fred, what would you like to do in this place?'

'I have no desire to be famous. Only useful. I thought perhaps a select committee . . .'

'How about I make you our housing spokesman?'

'Housing? I don't know the first thing about housing.'

'Oh, you could learn it all up . . .' That was the thing about clever people: they thought politics could be learned.

'I'm not sure I—'

'Of course you could. Anyway, it's only for a year or two and then I'll find you something more up your street – in the foreign affairs team perhaps. Are we agreed, then?' She awarded him one of her steely smiles. Already she was rising from her seat. Before he knew it he was out in the corridor, wondering what Elizabeth would have to say.

* * *

'How could you?' Elizabeth almost screamed, when he broke the news. 'Don't you think we've got enough on our plate?' Alone all day with little else to think about, Catherine's illness was wearing her down. The children were her life.

Catherine took to calling her tumour Malfoy, after a villain in her Harry Potter books. The name soon caught on. 'How's Malfoy today?' they would ask each morning and the little nugget would either whisper 'Malfoy's bad today' or later, when the medication took hold, she might remark that Malfoy had disappeared. 'I don't know where he's gone.'

Very soon there was to be an operation. 'Will it hurt?' she asked when they broke the news.

'No, darling. They will put you to sleep for a little while and while you are sleeping they will remove the lump on your brain. After that Malfoy will disappear.'

'But my brain is inside my head. How will they get in *there*?'

Hesitation. 'They will make a tiny hole.'

'A hole?'

'Only a little one. It will soon heal. And when you wake up, you'll feel much better.'

He turned away so that she couldn't see the tears in his eyes.

* * *

That night there were reports that a Chinese warship had fired a torpedo across the bows of the USS *George W. Bush*. Radio Beijing described it as a warning shot.

NINE

Catherine's operation went as well as could be expected. The bad news was that the tumour was malignant, but the surgeon was confident he had removed it all. 'We caught it early,' he said. 'The prognosis is good.'

'Is my brain still there?' was her first question on regaining consciousness. She had tubes attached to her nose, chest and right arm, plugged into a big machine by her bed, and one arm round Clarence, her favourite teddy bear.

'Yes, my darling.'

'And did they make a hole in my head?'

'Yes, but it's very small.'

'Can you see it?'

'No, it's all covered up. It will soon heal.'

She smiled and drifted back to sleep. Wisps of blond hair peeping from beneath the bandage around her little head, cuddling Clarence, whose head was also bandaged. He shared her pain.

* * *

Gradually life began to return to normal. For the first time in weeks Thompson attended the Friends' dinner in the upper room in Soho. He arrived late to find them discussing what line to take on the looming war with China. 'We shouldn't be under any illusions about China,' Jock Steeples was saying, 'it's an imperial power.'

'So is America,' said Stephen Carter.

'Maybe, but for once the Americans are on the side of the angels.'

'Angels is putting it a bit strongly. Declaring war over a few uninhabited islands, whether they belong to Japan or not, is utterly reckless.'

'Fact is,' said Steeples, 'the US has a treaty with Japan and has to be seen to uphold it, otherwise it will be Vietnam next and then Taiwan. The Chinese have claims on just about the entire East Sea – everything down to Malaysia. Of course,' he added, 'it helps that, this time around at least, the leader of the free world is not a complete moron.'

'Anyway, there's not much we can do about it,' said Mrs Cook, flashing him another of her steely smiles. 'Except sit tight and pray.'

* * *

Three days later the Chinese announced what their foreign minister described as 'a temporary suspension' of their operations in the East Sea, but he took care to reiterate his country's territorial claims. The US president, in a broadcast to the nation, adopted a notably conciliatory tone. He had always known, he said, that the Chinese were a peace-loving people. The US fleet would be withdrawing to its base in the Philippines.

'Just shows it pays to stand up to the bastards,' boomed Farquar when Fred encountered him in the library corridor.

The world breathed a sigh of relief, but no one thought this was the end of the matter. 'My guess is they'll go for Vietnam next,' said Steeples. 'The US has no treaty with the Vietnamese.'

* * *

A course of radiotherapy lay ahead. 'What's radiotherapy?' asked Catherine when they broke the news. The unfamiliar word rolled slowly from her tongue.

'They take you to a special room in the hospital. You lie on a bed. They put a mask over your head with a hole in just where the tumour was and then a big machine fires invisible rays at the spot where you were operated on to stop Malfoy coming back.'

'But I thought they took him out.'

'They did, but you don't want him coming back, do you?' Elizabeth turned away and brushed a tear from her eye.

'Why are you crying, Mummy?'

'Because I love you so much.'

TEN

Little Sunshine didn't make it.

At first she seemed to be recovering well from the long and debilitating bouts of radiotherapy. Her silky blond hair, most of which had fallen out, began to reappear. Colour gradually returned to her cheeks. She sang songs, resumed her piano lessons. When summer came Fred took a month off and they went back to their island. She and Lucy paddled and splashed in the sea. They explored rock pools, counted the seabirds, went seal-spotting and laid the foundations for a Stone Age house on the beach. And each evening she read Harry Potter aloud to her little sister. It was a golden summer. Old folk on the island said they could not recall a better one. Fred, Elizabeth and Lucy would remember that summer for the rest of their lives.

Come September, Catherine returned to school. After

long absence she had fallen behind, but with help from Elizabeth soon caught up. At first glance she was as care-free as ever, except that she now treated schoolwork with a new seriousness and often spent the evenings reading. 'When I grow up, I am going to be a brain doctor,' she said.

For a while all was well. The dark cloud that had hung over the family lifted. When parliament resumed Fred returned to work with a spring in his step. Elizabeth, too, was happier than she had been for a long time. The hollow eyes and the nervous tic that had appeared in her left temple disappeared. She and Fred were getting on better than they had done in ages. They graced the odd dinner party, went occasionally to the cinema and once to a performance of *The Messiah* by the parliament choir. They even resumed their lovemaking, which had been on hold since that dreadful day of the diagnosis.

***

In the House Fred was a rising star on the opposition front bench. He focused on the rise of the buy-to-let landlord, of whom there were not a few on the government benches and (if truth be told) one or two in the opposition ranks. He painted the housing crisis as yet another of the bills coming in for the Thatcher decade. At the very mention of their hero's name the pinstripes on the government benches rose like a lot of Pavlov dogs. 'Will the honourable gentleman give way?'

Fred ploughed on. The cries of 'give way' intensified. He looked around, his eyes alighting upon Jason Joslin – J. J. to his friends – a smug young man of modest origins who had, by fair means or foul, clawed his way to considerable wealth. Witness the Armani suit and the gold cufflinks that protruded a full three inches from the sleeves of his jacket.

'I give way.'

'The honourable gentleman traduces a woman whose shoelaces he is not fit to tie,' snorted Joslin. Cue much harrumphing on the benches behind him. 'Is he aware that, as the child of a single parent, brought up on one of London's toughest council estates, I and thousands like me reared in similar circumstances owe everything we have to the achievements of Margaret Thatcher's government?'

Thompson eyed the foe carefully, evincing an air of distaste even before he had uttered a word in reply. 'I have no doubt,' he said slowly, 'that the honourable gentleman and others who worship at the shrine of Blessed Margaret owe her a great deal.' Pause. 'It's just a pity that they have kicked away the ladder up which they have climbed.'

Cue cheers from the opposition benches and cries of 'disgraceful' from the benches opposite, although one or two patricians seemed to be quietly smirking behind their order papers. Jason Joslin was not universally popular on his own side.

'Well done, my boy. Bull's eye,' whispered Farquar when their paths briefly crossed in the library corridor that evening. 'Come and see me in Lord North Street this evening, after the division. I have some information that you might find of interest.'

* * *

'Ah there you are, dear boy.' Farquar, once more resplendent in his velvet smoking jacket, opened the door. 'Come in, come in.'

Once again Fred was ushered up the narrow staircase past the *Vanity Fair* prints into the panelled first-floor drawing room, illuminated only by two large lamps and a spotlight over the fireplace.

'Do sit down.' Farquar indicated a well-worn winged armchair, one of a pair on either side of the empty grate. They had seen better days. In several places the stuffing was exposed. Funny how the upper classes never seemed to bother about wear and tear. In a working-class household chairs like that would have gone to the dump years ago. Farquar seemed to read Fred's thoughts. 'Been in the family for years, they have. Belonged to my great-grandfather who was in Lord Salisbury's cabinet.

Legend has it that Salisbury actually sat exactly where you are now.'

Ah, that explained it.

'Whisky?'

'Thank you.'

Farquar poured them both a generous measure.

'Ice?

'Please.'

He made himself comfortable in the opposite armchair. 'How's your daughter? Terrible business that. You've had a hard time.'

'Fingers crossed. She's back at school. Life's returned to normal, more or less.' Fred's voice trailed off. 'But of course you never know.'

'No, I don't suppose you do. Well, here's to her health.' Farquar raised his glass.

A moment's silence, interrupted only by the clock of St John's in Smith Square striking the hour. Farquar sipped his whisky. He seemed in no hurry to get to the point. His demeanour was gloomy. 'Brexit not working out too well, is it? Do you think, if we ask nicely, the Europeans will let us back?'

'I very much doubt it. They seem glad to be rid of us.'

'Thatcher – that woman's got a lot to answer for. All this anti-Europe nonsense started on her watch. Instead of stamping on it she positively encouraged it.' He stared morosely into his whisky. 'Flogging off the family silver didn't work out too well either. Some of us did try to warn her, but she wasn't listening. Now look where we are. A second-rate power going on third-rate. The gap between top and bottom wider than ever. Our party flooded with all these so-called self-made wide boys like Flather and Joslin. Self-made, my foot. They've never made anything useful in their lives.'

Another long silence. The headlights from a passing car briefly flickered across the ceiling. 'Well, my boy, I've got something for you. After our little success with that bastard Flather who, by the way, comes up at the Old Bailey next week. Suppose you know that, don't you?'

'Actually, I didn't. A bit preoccupied of late. I'm slightly surprised. Thought I might be asked to give evidence.'

'Apparently he's pleading guilty, which will save everyone a lot of trouble. Slippery bugger though. I bet he's done some sort of deal. Even so, the word is that he'll go down. Couldn't happen to a nicer fellow.' A malicious grin drifted across Farquar's ample features. He reached for a thin beige file which lay on the floor at his feet. 'Anyway, to business.' He passed the file. 'Have a look at this.'

The file contained a dozen sheets of paper relating to a property company called St Margaret's Housing Trust. '*Saint* Margaret, forsooth. These spivs are taking the mickey.' Three directors were listed: Jason Charles Joslin and Cynthia Michelle Joslin, both of the same address in Pimlico, and one Richard Lloyd Cathcart whose address was given as an apartment in the Barbican. 'Cynthia is his wife, a hard-faced bleached blonde, also employed as his secretary in the Commons, another effing scam. Cathcart is some sort of shady City wallah.'

'What does this company do?'

'Housing, of course. For rental, not purchase.'

'How many properties do they have?'

'Look at the bottom three sheets, there's a list. I had someone go through the Land Registry.'

'Goodness, there's a lot.'

'A hundred and forty-eight, to be precise.'

'And mainly in the same three or four blocks, by the looks of things.'

'Ex-local authority houses. Every one. And in the same borough. Two of the blocks are in prime sites, overlooking the river. In one eight-storey building, the trust owns more than half the flats, all purchased under the right to buy at huge discounts. Apparently by tenants, but I happen to know that Joslin and Cathcart usually put up the money. The terms of the purchase require the tenant to remain there for five years, after which they can do what they like. At that point Joslin usually buys them out and the properties are re-let at much higher rents, often to foreigners.'

'All strictly legal, I take it'?

'More or less. Sometimes pressure is applied on tenants who don't want to sell. Known in the trade as winkling, I believe. Can be a bit nasty sometimes. There was an incident ten years ago, just before Joslin was elected, that made a few paragraphs in the papers but it was all smoothed over. A misunderstanding, it was said.'

Farquar walked over to the drinks cabinet and refilled their glasses. He raised his glass.

'There we are, dear boy. All yours. A rich treasure trove. Requires a little footwork, of course, but nothing you can't handle. Just keep my name out of it, that's all.'

* * *

Early next morning Catherine came to their bedroom. Tears on her cheeks, a hand pressed to the left side of her head. 'Mummy, Daddy, my head hurts. I think Malfoy has come back.'

ELEVEN

For a while they pretended that this was just a temporary setback and for a while Catherine pretended to believe them. Then out of the blue one day, a month after the tumour reappeared, she said, 'Dad, do you know about heaven?'

'Yes, darling.'

'We learned about it at school. It's a place where good people go. There's music and fun and laughter and everybody's happy.'

A tear welled in his eye. It was one of Catherine's good days. They were in the park, watching children on the swings.

'Do you know where heaven is, Dad?'

'No, darling.'

'It's up there in the sky,' she pointed to a large white cloud. And then, 'Do you believe in heaven, Dad?'

'Of course, my sunshine,' he lied.

'Did you know there are angels in heaven? With wings and shiny faces and they can fly.'

'Who told you that'?

'Our teacher, Mrs Morgan. Her sister died and she said she was going to see her again one day, in heaven.'

He hugged her close so she couldn't see the tears streaming down his face.

* * *

By now they had given up the lease at Edale and moved into Elizabeth's parents' first-floor flat in Chelsea. It was spacious. Three bedrooms, a large sitting room, shared use of a small garden. Above all, it was close to the hospital.

There followed more hospital visits, another scan, another debilitating course of chemotherapy, whispered conversations with doctors and nurses, much shaking of heads and discreet tears, before finally an acceptance that it was hopeless.

Meanwhile Catherine grew paler and weaker. There were days when she felt well enough to dress herself and sit reading by the window, watching people going by in the street below. Once or twice she even asked to go to school and they took her, only to have to collect her again when after a few hours she became too tired.

They borrowed a wheelchair from the Red Cross and one sunny day took her on a boat ride from Westminster pier to Kew.

'Oooh look, Dad, there's your parliament.' She always referred to it as 'your parliament' or 'Dad's parliament', as though Thompson owned the place.

They waved and the people on the terrace waved back. His visits to parliament were becoming infrequent; he had not set foot in the chamber for six weeks. His front bench colleagues were understanding, and lately the whips had given him leave of absence. Once a week he caught the train to Sheffield, did his surgeries, fulfilled a few local engagements, but he was only going through the motions. 'How's the little person doing?' people would ask. They meant well, but he wished they wouldn't ask. Eventually, the enquiries stopped.

That boat trip was her last proper outing. Gradually the good days became rarer. The drugs she was pre-scribed made her drowsier. Each evening, after school, Lucy would race to the bedroom and climb into bed with her sister. A touching little scene. They would lie together, arms around each other, watching Harry Potter videos with Clarence the teddy bear propped up between them. More often than not Catherine had nodded off before the end.

Elizabeth's mother came to stay. Sitting with Catherine

and telling stories about life in the old days. The days when there were no Harry Potter videos, houses were lit by candles and oil lamps, ladies wore tight corsets and dresses that came down to their ankles, and when rich people had servants in white caps and pinafores and travelled in horse-drawn carriages.

Elizabeth dug out the family photo albums and they would leaf through pictures of the good times they had on what they called 'our island'. Lucy and Catherine playing on the beach. Building what they called their Stone Age house. Drawing faces in the sand with moustaches made of seaweed.

'We were so happy there,' said the little person. 'Maybe if we hadn't moved away I wouldn't have Malfoy in my head.'

'We'll go again, just as soon you're well enough,' they said, but they could see she didn't believe them.

* * *

Little Sunshine slipped away on a bright spring day when the local park was alive with daffodils and pink blossom on the cherry trees.

Outside their front door life had been going on as normal. Each morning in the street below, tiny school persons in smart uniforms, oblivious to the cares of the world, scootered along the pavement, their mothers scurrying to keep up. In the evening, from the direction of the park, childish laughter. Every fifteen minutes or so a bus passed by on its way to Sloane Square. In quieter moments, from the direction of the river, the sound of a helicopter or a low-flying plane on its way to Heathrow was briefly audible. And always the low hum of traffic. Gradually, however, external noise was filtered out and the apartment became a silent place whose inhabitants crept from room to room, communicating with each other in morose whispers, occasionally embracing wordlessly. Towards the end curtains remained drawn as if no one wanted to be reminded that in the world outside there was sunshine and happiness.

Day and night they took turns to sit with her, clutching a pale, lifeless hand – Granny, Grandpa, Fred, Elizabeth, Lucy and, in the final days, a succession of Macmillan nurses. For the last week she did not eat, sitting up occasionally to sip water. Morphine was administered through a drip attached to her arm. Her little face, radiant to the end, wreathed in blond curls, grew thinner and paler.

'Daddy, I can see angels,' she whispered as she drifted in and out of consciousness on the last day.

It was more than Fred could bear. Tears streamed down his face. 'Oh please don't go, Little Sunshine. Please stay with us. Please, please stay.'

'Don't be upset, Daddy. They have very kind faces. They will look after me.'

That was the last thing she said.

* * *

The funeral was at St Luke's on Sydney Street. By request it was a small affair, family and close friends only. Elizabeth's parents, a couple of aunts, a handful of neighbours. From Fred's side, no relatives. Parents long gone. A stepsister last heard of five years back in Australia. The Labour Party was his family: Jock Steeples, Mrs Cook and Stephen Carter, his closest friends in parliament. Vera Clarke and Ronnie Morgan from Sheffield. From Catherine's school, teachers, classmates and the choir, two dozen little shiny-faced people in their smart blue uniforms. The little white coffin, topped with daffodils cut that morning from her grandparents' garden, entered the church followed by her distraught parents and her tiny sister, Lucy, clutching Clarence the teddy bear who still had his head bandaged.

The priest, a lady vicar, read a prayer and kept her homily mercifully brief. What is there to say about the death of a much-loved child? A golden little life snuffed out. That it is God's will? What kind of God would be so cruel?

The choir, of which Catherine had been a member, sang 'All Things Bright and Beautiful'. Mrs Morgan, her class teacher, paid a short tribute and read a poem.

'I'll lend you for a little time a child of
    mine,' He said,
'For you to love the while she lives and mourn
    for when she's dead.
It may be six or seven years, or twenty-
    two or three,
But will you, till I call her back, take care of
    her for Me?
She'll bring her charm to gladden you and,
    should her stay be brief,
You'll have her lovely memories as solace for
    your grief.'

Thompson, in a trembling voice, gave a brief account of that golden little life, speculating on what might have been, and concluding, 'If I live to be a hundred there will not be a day,' a pause to regain composure, 'perhaps not a single hour in a single day . . .' another pause, 'when I do not see that shiny face smiling up at me.' Then, head down, he returned to his seat, the silence broken only by the sound of sobbing.

Later, at the crematorium, the little coffin disappeared

to the sound of Westlife singing 'Queen of My Heart', a song that, in happier times, they used to sing together as they drove up the motorway to Sheffield.

* * *

Come Whitsun they returned to 'their' island and scattered the little person's ashes on a grassy hill overlooking the beach on which she had once played. 'Daddy,' asked Lucy, as they walked back to the cottage, 'will we ever be happy again?'

TWELVE

A few days after the funeral a Macmillan nurse came and took away the medicines, the wheelchair, the drip and various other paraphernalia that had helped Catherine through her last days. Thompson returned to work and Elizabeth busied herself looking after Lucy and volunteering three days a week at a food bank in Battersea. It was a month before they could bring themselves to set foot in Catherine's room. The curtains remained drawn and the door firmly closed. Clarence the teddy bear had moved in with Lucy, but that apart, Catherine's possessions remained untouched. One morning, after Elizabeth had delivered Lucy to school, they finally plucked up the courage to open the door and entered hand in hand. The room, in twilight, was just as the little person had left it. As if she had gone away and would be back in a few days. The Cinderella duvet was pulled up over the pillows, her boy band posters still on the wall, the bookshelf with the complete works of Harry Potter, framed photographs of Granny and Grandpa and the four of them outside their whitewashed cottage, taken on their last visit to 'their' island. 'I can smell her,' Elizabeth said quietly as she drew back the curtains.

'How long are we going to leave it like this?'

'It's too early yet.'

'Sooner or later we will have to let go.'

'Yes,' said Elizabeth quietly.

'At least we should put the sheets in the wash.'

Elizabeth began to strip the bed. She lifted a pillow, 'What's this?'

It was an envelope, addressed in Catherine's large, childish hand. It read, 'MY WILL'. With trembling hands Elizabeth opened it and, without looking, handed the note inside to Fred. In a quavering voice he read it aloud, '*I leave Clarence my teddy bear to Lucy. Also my Harry Potter DVDs. To Dad I leave my collection of coloured stones. To Mum my Westlife CDs and the scrapbook we made together. Everything els I leave to the poor children in Africa exsept my Pokeman cards which I leave to Daniel in my class at school. Signed Catherine Thompson*' and sealed with a smiley face. It was dated five days before her death.

* * *

Two more weeks elapsed before Thompson could bring himself to attend another meeting of the Friends. 'Welcome back, Fred,' said Jock Steeples. 'A lot's happened while you've been away.' Several of the others shook his hand warmly and one or two tapped him gently on the shoulders. Mrs Cook gave him a hug and Molly Spence planted a kiss on his cheek.

The previous week Michael Flather had pleaded guilty at the Old Bailey to people trafficking. He had been sent down for nine years. Albert the driver had got off with a suspended sentence in the light of his co-operation. Rosemary Eames had been interviewed, but the prosecution had decided there was not enough evidence to charge her. After the trial Thompson had been besieged by requests for interviews, but contented himself with a short statement saying only that he was glad to see justice done.

'A good result,' said Mrs Cook.

'Aye,' said Steeples, 'this won't do you any harm at all. You're respectable now.'

'What are you going to do for an encore?' asked Stephen Carter.

'As it happens, I do have something up my sleeve,' said Thompson, fleetingly more chipper than he had felt for a long while.

* * *

An opposition day debate was easily arranged. The shadow cabinet agreed that Thompson would lead. It would be his first appearance on the front bench in four months. A handful of favoured journalists were briefed in strict confidence. In accordance with the usual courtesies, Thompson at the last moment dropped a handwritten note to Jason Joslin MP, advising him that he was likely to be named, and there he was in his usual seat in the back row of the government benches looking a shade less self-satisfied than usual, fidgeting with his notes, nervously flicking back his long blond hair. Already he looked an isolated figure. His colleagues seemed to have left a wide space around him. Almost as if they anticipated that he was about to become untouchable. No doubt the fate of Michael Flather was fresh in their minds.

As was his habit Thompson warmed up slowly. No hyperbole, no synthetic indignation, just a calm setting out of the facts. The country, he said, was facing an unprecedented housing crisis. A vast and widening gulf had opened between an older generation, most of whom had been able to afford their own their homes, and a younger generation – the so-called Generation Rent – most of whom had not the slightest hope of buying their own homes, unless they had parents who could afford to subsidise them. This problem was particularly acute in London and the south-east. Local authorities which had once provided homes for those unable to afford their own, could now no longer do so. They had been obliged to sell off much of their housing stock at knock-down prices and forbidden – yes *forbidden* – to use the proceeds to build more. As a result many young families had been forced into private rented accommodation, much of it substandard.

'I do not wish to exaggerate, Madam Speaker. There is no single cause, but there is one aspect of this crisis in particular upon which I wish to focus today: the rise of a particularly venal species, the buy-to-let landlord.' He glanced at Joslin who shifted uneasily in his seat. 'The sale of local authority housing was sold to us, back in the heady days of the Thatcher ascendancy, on the basis that it would extend home ownership to those who might not otherwise be able to afford it.'

'Would the honourable gentleman give way?' It was the housing minister, an amiable cove by the name of Tristram Bellweather. In a previous incarnation he had been the managing director of an upmarket firm of estate agents.

'Certainly.'

'Is it not a fact that the sale of council houses repre-sented a huge redistribution of wealth to some of our least prosperous citizens, who hitherto had not been able to benefit from rising house prices?' This triggered a bout of hear-hearing from pinstripes on the government benches. Bellweather, glowing with self-satisfaction, resumed his seat.

Thompson surveyed the serried ranks. 'Good to know,' he said, 'that the honourable gentlemen opposite believe in the redistribution of wealth.' Cue derisive laughter from the opposition benches. 'Unfortunately, in this case, most of the redistribution that took place was not at the expense of those who owned the wealth, but at the expense of the next generation who now find themselves excluded from public sector housing and consigned to the tender mercies of the private landlord.' Cue raucous cheering from the opposition benches and cries of 'nonsense' from the government side. And then, 'I don't think the sale of public housing had anything to do with redistributing wealth. I think it was about bribing the electorate.'

Uproar. Cries of 'disgraceful' and 'withdraw'. Thompson ploughed on.

'Madam Speaker, today I wish to focus on one particularly perverse outcome from the enforced sale of public housing. It is an unhappy fact that many of those who have benefited from this disastrous policy are not the former council tenants who exercised their right to buy. They have long ago moved on. No, the stark reality is that many former council properties have been hoovered up by buy-to-let landlords. We do not have far to look for examples ...' Out of the corner of his eye Thompson noticed

Rupert Farquar lurking in the shadows by the entrance to the aye lobby. 'We are fortunate to have with us today the honourable member for Uxford who, together with his wife and a gentleman named Richard Lloyd Cathcart, owns no fewer than 148 former council properties, most of them in a single London borough.'

More uproar. More cries of 'disgraceful'. Demands for points of order. The speaker was on her feet.

'I hope the honourable gentleman has evidence for that assertion.'

'I do indeed, Madam Speaker. In fact I have a little list.' He waved a sheaf of papers.

Jason Joslin was on his feet, red-faced with anger. Thompson gave way.

'What precisely is the honourable gentleman alleging? The House should be aware that I run a perfectly legitimate business.'

'I trust the honourable gentleman does. I am not alleging any impropriety. I am merely seeking to place on record a state of affairs that many people, of all political persuasions, may find remarkable. So far as I am aware, it was never part of the plan that the sale of public housing should enrich the likes of the honourable gentleman and a handful of his friends. And if that was the intention, no one mentioned it at the time.'

* * *

No one spoke up for Joslin. He fled the chamber pursued by journalists and the following day found himself splashed across the front pages. A week later he was the subject of a *Panorama* special. The suggestion that some of the tenants who had been persuaded to sell to St Margaret's Housing Trust might have been pressured into doing so began to resurface. It turned out that the mysterious Mr Cathcart had a bit of a track record when it came to persuading those who had exercised their right to buy to sell up. What's more, it emerged that in a number cases – actually quite a few – Joslin and Cathcart had put up the money that enabled them to exercise their right to buy. There was talk of a police investigation and rumours of an uprising in the Uxford Conservative Association.

In the months that followed, Thompson's star rose. Seldom had a newcomer made such an impact in so short a time. Even the old codgers in the tea room warmed to him. The Tories, too, had him marked down as a man to watch. Two months after the fall of Joslin he was made shadow foreign secretary. Suddenly the world was his oyster.

Thirteen

But no triumph was so great that it could erase the memory of Little Sunshine. First thing in the morning and last thing at night, and on many occasions during the day, he saw that shiny face smiling at him. He saw her as he walked to work along the Embankment. He saw her on the swings in Victoria Tower Gardens. Sometimes he found himself talking to her. *'Come back, Sunny. I'll give all this up and we'll go back and live on our island and be happy again.'* Sometimes he imagined her talking to him. *'Well done, Dad,'* she said after his promotion, *'You're going to be famous one day.'*

* * *

FRED THOMPSON IS A USELESS TWAT. Mrs Jeffries came in one morning to find this painted in large white letters across the plate glass of Thompson's constituency office. Thomas Merton was the obvious suspect, but there was no evidence, and anyway there were a number of other candidates. Merton had not been seen or heard of for weeks. Maybe he had read about Catherine and deep inside that thick skull there was some sliver of decency. Even so, after consulting the police, Thompson decided to take precautions. Metal shutters were installed on the front and rear windows along with discreet panic alarms in both the outer office and the inner sanctum.

* * *

'Statement. The foreign secretary,' intoned the speaker. Sir Francis Oswald rose. His demeanour was grave. A gent of the old school, he had somehow, miraculously, survived into the third decade of the twenty-first century. A hereditary baronet. His wife the daughter of a duke, related to half the statues in the Foreign Office. The twenty-fifth, or so it was said, member of his dynasty to sit in the Commons. Civilised, gentlemanly, unfailingly courteous. One of a dying breed who did his best, not always successfully, to conceal his distaste for the estate agents, hedge funders and barrow boys who increasingly populated the benches behind him. They, in turn, resented him as a relic of the old order. 'Madam Speaker, I very much regret to inform the House that His Majesty's government have decided to relinquish our permanent seat on the Security Council of the United Nations. We have done so with the greatest reluctance, but as the House will be aware the UN secretary general has expressed a wish to reform the composition of the Security Council, so that it better reflects the balance of power in the modern world. Regretfully, it has been apparent for some time that we no longer enjoy the support of other permanent members. It is proposed that India replace the United Kingdom and that the European Union, of which of course we are no longer a member, will have two seats, which are likely in the first instance to be occupied by France and Germany ...' His words were drowned by uproar on the benches behind him. From the opposition benches, a stony silence and much shaking of heads.

'Mr Fred Thompson.'

His first outing as foreign affairs spokesman, but he could hardly have hoped for a more open goal. Every successful politician needs luck, and it was becoming increasingly apparent to friend and foe alike that Thompson was a lucky politician.

'Madam Speaker, no one in this House should be surprised by this most regrettable announcement. We are one of the founder members of the United Nations. We have been a leading member since its inception. Is this not the clearest possible evidence of the depths to which our nation has sunk since the right honourable gentleman's party, in one of its periodic bouts of insanity, decided to lead this country into the wilderness?' Sir Francis's face assumed a pained expression. None of this was his doing. Indeed behind the scenes he had fought a long rearguard action, but it had come to naught. He was rumoured to be on the brink of resignation. 'Will the foreign secretary confirm that this is yet another of the bills coming in for Brexit? Will he confirm that not even our old ally the United States stuck up for us? Is he not ashamed of the damage his party has done to our standing in the world? When will he find the courage to face up to the zealots in his party who have brought this country to its present pass?'

Thompson sat down to cheers from the opposition benches and a stunned silence from the government side. Sir Francis did his best to respond robustly, but it was obvious to all that his heart wasn't in it. There followed an hour in which he was assailed from all sides. From the government benches much harrumphing at the wickedness of it all, the perfidy of foreigners in general and the United Nations in particular. The news that Germany – *Germany* of all countries – would replace the UK on the Security Council was a source of particular apoplexy. There was anger too that the US government had not come to our aid. So much for the much-vaunted 'special relationship'. Several of the new breed of Tories demanded that the British contribution to UN funding be drastically cut. One or two even went so far as to demand British withdrawal. Stephen Carter had the last word. 'Have you noticed, Madam Speaker, that those who are loudest in their outrage are also those who were most voluble in their demand that Britain should leave the EU? What did they expect?'

* * *

'Well done, son,' said Jock Steeples when the Friends reconvened a week later in their upper room in Soho. 'You're turning into a bit of a star. I reckon you're leadership material.' His words prompted a mild bout of hear-hearing from around the table. Mrs Cook raised her glass. Others followed.

'Steady on,' said Thompson, 'aren't we getting a bit ahead of ourselves?'

'On the contrary,' said Steeples, 'it's time to get serious. Having lost five general elections in succession, we can't afford to take any chances on the outcome of a sixth. Even now we are little more than level pegging in the polls. Given the mess they've got us into, we should be streets ahead.'

'You are not suggesting some sort of coup?

'That's precisely what I am suggesting.'

'After 125 years the dear old Labour Party has just got round to electing our first female leader and you want me to try and remove her?'

'Why not? She's hopeless. Pleasant, yes. Intelligent, yes. But entirely lacking in passion or charisma.. We're heading for yet another defeat. You know that as well as I do.'

'I'm surprised at you, Jock,' said Mrs Cook indignantly. 'You've been around long enough to know that Labour never removes failing leaders. We go down with the ship.'

'Yeah,' said Steeples, 'and it's about time we kicked the habit.'

'Even if she were removed,' added Stephen Carter, 'there's no guarantee that our candidate would end up in the driving seat.'

'Plus,' added Mrs Cook, 'we'd have to cope with a party that was hopelessly divided. It took the Tories ten years to recover from removing Thatcher.'

It was apparent that there were no takers and Steeples didn't press the point. The discussion petered out and they fell back upon a well-worn theme: the fallout from Brexit, devaluation, the growing trade deficit. 'Surely,' remarked Molly Spence, 'the Great British Public will sooner or later notice that Brexit isn't working?'

'They may well do,' said Anne-Marie Freeman, the

Times columnist, 'but it doesn't follow they will turn to Labour.'

'What's the alternative?'

'Fascism.' Ms Freeman did not often intervene in their deliberations, but when she did she tended to have the final word.

* * *

The election came earlier than expected, pre-empting any further talk of coups. It turned out that the Great British Public were not that bothered by the loss of the British seat on the Security Council. Nor had many of them – at least those who were unfamiliar with 'abroad' – noticed the declining value of the currency. What they had noticed – indeed it was repeatedly drawn to their attention by much of our free press – was that there had been a steep decline in the number of foreign migrants. This was a card played with great zeal by the governing party. No matter that it reflected a reduction in the number of foreign students or that the fall in overseas nurses and doctors was the cause of a growing crisis in the NHS. There were fewer foreigners and that's what mattered. The outcome was yet another Tory triumph, albeit by a narrower margin than previously.

'What did I tell you?' remarked Elizabeth as the last

results trickled in. 'All this politicking is a complete waste of time. We live in a one-party state and that's that. Time you gave up and did something useful.'

'And what might that be? Ex-MPs, particularly ex-Labour MPs, are virtually unemployable these days.'

'Oh you'd find something. Why don't you write a biography of Harry, like you've been promising to do for the last five years? There would be a market for that, surely.'

'Maybe, but it would be a five-minute wonder. What would I do after that? I don't think I could bear being unemployed in middle age.'

Elizabeth sighed deeply and closed her eyes. Deep down she knew he was right. Anyway, if truth be told, it wasn't Fred who needed something useful to do, it was her. There had to be more to life than ferrying Lucy to and from school and volunteering at a food bank.

* * *

An envelope arrived, addressed in a spidery hand to 'Frederick Thompson Esq.'. In the top left-hand corner, in the same spidery hand, were the words 'strictly personal'. Unusually, it was delivered to his home address. It stood out because in these days of digital media so few people, most of them elderly, communicated by letter. The stamp was first class and the just-about-legible postmark suggested it had been posted in Somerset. He opened it cautiously, using a kitchen knife. Inside was a single handwritten sheet topped by a printed address, 'Quantock Manor'. The message, in a scrawl that was barely legible, was brief. It read as follows:

> *Dear Frederick (if I may),*
>
> *I have followed with great interest your progress in public life and I believe you have a great future. As you can see from my rickety hand, I am getting on a bit now and wondered if we might meet up before I finally kick the bucket. Don't get up to London these days so, assuming you are willing, I must prevail upon you to visit me down here. To arrange an appointment please call the above number.*
>
> *My warmest regards,*
> *Peregrine Craddock*

* * *

'Well I never, the cheeky old rascal,' remarked Mrs Cook when Fred showed her the letter that evening in the tea room.

'What do you reckon he wants to talk to me about?'

'Goodness knows. Perhaps he wants to confess his many sins.'

'Should I go?'

'Can't do any harm. Let me know how you get on.'

An appointment was duly arranged.

* * *

A sign on the gatepost stated firmly, in solid black block capitals, that this place was PRIVATE, though the gate was open. The drive was long and winding, through an avenue of ancient oaks which eventually parted to reveal a crumbling mansion, mullioned windows, trailing wisteria and a sundial on which the date 1615 was just legible. The house nestled in a small valley between low wooded hills.

The porch contained a swallow's nest. A bell with a frayed rope attached hung from a rusting bracket. Thompson rang and waited. Nothing happened. He rang again and eventually faint footsteps could be heard from within. The door was opened by a stout, elderly woman in a light blue housecoat. The housekeeper, he thought at first glance, but it turned out to be Lady Craddock. She shook his hand firmly. 'Sorry to drag you all the way down here, but Perry is rather frail these days. He has been looking forward to your visit. Perked him up no end, it has. He's waiting for you in the library.'

She led him through the hall, along a dark passageway, and into an oak-panelled room, lined along one side from floor to ceiling with books. 'Perry, it's your visitor, Mr Thompson.'

He was seated in a wheelchair by double doors which opened out onto a small terrace; sunlight streamed through, a copy of *The Times*, half open, lay at his feet. 'Ah, dear boy, so good of you to come.' He made as if to rise, but the effort was too great and he fell back into the chair, emaciated right hand extended for Thompson to shake.

'Can I get you a drink, Mr Thompson? And something to eat perhaps? You've come a long way.' They settled on a cheese and pickle sandwich and a glass of peppermint tea. Sir Peregrine said he'd have the same. With that Lady Craddock disappeared.

'Lovely place you've got here.'

'Yes, isn't it? Badly in need of repair, I'm afraid. Like its owner. In the family for 300 years. Not sure what will become of it after we go. Neither of my two boys interested. Damn pity, but what can one do?'

Sir Peregrine's glasses hung by a string (or was it a shoelace?) from his neck. He looked very much as he had always done: a good head of grey hair, the same boyish, soft pink cheeks, bushy eyebrows. He still spoke in the same clipped tones. 'Not very mobile these days. Old age terrible. Don't recommend.'

Lady Craddock appeared with the sandwiches and two mugs of peppermint tea. Sir Peregrine's she placed on a small table which folded down on the front of his wheel-chair, Thompson's on a mat on a small table beside his armchair. 'I think you know my nephew,' she said, 'Rupert Farquar. He speaks very highly of you.'

'Yes, I like him, too.'

'A good boy. Chip off the old block. Out of place in the modern Conservative Party, I'm afraid. Probably has more in common with your lot than the present management.'

'Yes,' said Thompson weakly, not wanting to reveal the full extent of his collaboration with Farquar.

'Anyway, I'll leave you to Perry. It's him you've come to see.' And with that she disappeared into the gloomy interior.

* * *

'First, I wanted to say how dreadfully sorry I am about Harry. Greatest regret of my life. Decent man. Always knew that, but naive. So naive.'

'Naive about what?'

'To imagine the Americans would let him get away with chucking out their bases. The other stuff, House of Lords, public schools, he could probably have got away with, but not the bases.'

'Don't you think you ought to have left it to the electorate?'

121

'Perhaps we should – these days we probably would. More important things to worry about. Islamist terror and all that. A different world then. Sterling an international currency and we were so heavily in debt to the Americans that they could have wrecked the economy if they'd set their mind to it.' He shook his head gloomily.

'And Trident?'

'Ah yes, Trident. A virility symbol, nothing more. Useless, except as a stick to beat your side with. The Americans never wanted us to have it in the first place. They were afraid that if we got the bomb the French and the Germans would want it, too. They were right about the French but not, thank God, about the Germans.' He smiled wearily.

'And expensive.'

'Oh yes, very. Madness, actually. Most of the military know that and so do the Tories. One day they will get up and announce they are going to phase out Trident. It will be a five-minute wonder and then forgotten. If I were you, I'd leave it to them, instead of banging on about it.'

Outside the sun was shining. A sprinkler played on the lawn, the water sparkling in the sunlight. 'Would you like to see the garden? You'll have to push me, I'm afraid. Legs no use these days. Such a bore.' They made their way cautiously to the open French windows, Fred manoeuvring the wheelchair slowly down a little ramp onto a stone patio beside a herbaceous border, not yet in full flower, and then to a winding path through the rose garden.

'My wife does most of it, though we have a chap who comes in twice a week to do the lawns and the heavy lifting.'

They had come to rest in a shaded arbour overlooking a pond in which white lilies floated.

'Very sorry to hear about your daughter, by the way. Saw a picture in the paper. Beautiful little person.'

'Yes.'

'I lost a daughter, too. Years ago. Aged fifteen. Killed by some idiot on a motorbike.'

'I'm sorry.'

'One never gets over the loss of a child. Think about her every day. Expect you do, too.'

'Yes.'

They sat in silence. A full minute passed.

'Used to be fish in the pond, but the heron took them. Tried putting a net over it, but that didn't seem to work either.'

* * *

They talked about China. Sir Peregrine was of the opinion that the dispute with Japan would blow over on the grounds that war wasn't in either country's interests. As for the Americans, they would back down, too.

They talked Brexit. To Thompson's pleasant surprise Sir Peregrine was of the view that the great falling out with the EU was a disaster which would sooner or later have to be reversed. 'Until the recent election I've voted Tory all my life, but I can't forgive them for the mess they've got us into. And the gap between rich and poor is getting too wide. You may be surprised to hear that a lot of my posh friends down here think that. It's gone too far.'

Another longish silence and then, 'Expect you are wondering why I asked you down here.'

'I did, rather.'

'I'll be frank. My friends in high places – oh yes, I still have a few – have high hopes of you. Not to put too fine a point on it, they think you could go all the way. And, if you get my drift, they don't want any repeat of previous misunderstandings.'

'Me neither.'

'I think I might be able to help you.'

'Oh yes?'

'I realise you may be sceptical in the light of previous experience, but believe me, a much more enlightened view prevails these days. On our side of the river, anyway. Can't speak for Vauxhall Cross. Still a few idiots there. Plus, of course, this EU business. The government have sold out the country just to satisfy a handful of zealots on their own side. For all that phony flag-waving they've done more damage to the national interest than your lot ever would have done.' His tone reeked of contempt. He was a man who felt badly let down. 'What I want to suggest is this. If your career progresses as I anticipate, and if you are serious about power, you will at least need to have a modus vivendi with my friends in high places. That's where I may be able to assist. But for God's sake get a move on, because I have a feeling I may not last much longer.'

* * *

That evening, as anticipated, Mrs Jones announced that, having presided over two successive election defeats, she was standing down as leader of the opposition. Her announcement prompted a good deal of *faux* dismay. Some immediately declared that she must be succeeded by another woman, but the general view was that in the circumstances winning would have to take priority over political correctness.

Fourteen

An emergency meeting of the Friends was convened. It took place in Mrs Cook's office on the third floor of Portcullis House, a corner room with a big bay window affording fine views over Parliament Square towards the Abbey. 'Well, son, it's now or never. Are you up for it?' enquired Jock Steeples.

A momentary hesitation and then, 'Yes.'

'You're sure?'

'Yes.'

'What about Elizabeth'? asked Mrs Cook.

'Not so keen, I'm afraid.' In fact, as Thompson well knew she would be utterly opposed.

'Is she persuadable?'

'I hope so. Perhaps you ought to talk to her.'

'If not Fred, who else is there?' asked Stephen Carter.

An awkward pause. 'How about Joan?' asked Thompson.

'Past my sell-by date, I'm afraid,' Mrs Cook said brightly.

'Seriously, you have a national profile, you've been home secretary.'

'That was yonks ago. Downhill all the way since then. No, it's got to be someone fresh and bright. On the way up, not on the way down. A new broom, and Fred's the only one we've got. Besides,' she added with a smile, 'I no longer have the necessary killer instinct.'

'And Fred does?'

'Oh yes. In spades.'

The meeting was adjourned to allow time for Elizabeth to be consulted. Thompson was dreading it. She would not be happy.

* * *

He broke the news next morning, after delivering Lucy to school. They were in the kitchen. Elizabeth, a mug of coffee in hand, was gazing out of the window at a posse of blue tits squabbling over a place on the bird feeder in their little garden.

She sighed deeply, 'Oh Fred, won't you ever learn?'

'Learn what?'

'That it's all a waste of time. The chances of a Labour government are low at the best of times. And even if it did happen, it will end in disappointment.'

'I can't accept that we are destined indefinitely to remain a one-party state.'

'But why does it have to be you?'

'It doesn't have to be me—'

'Then don't do it!' She slammed her coffee mug on the table so hard that the dregs splashed over the top.

'Odds are I won't get it anyway, but I'd never forgive myself if I didn't give it a try.'

'But you've given it a try once already. With Harry. And look how it ended.' She was almost shouting now.

'I am under a lot of pressure to run.'

'Pressure from whom? If you mean that fucking stupid little dining club of yours ...' It was unlike Elizabeth to swear.

'Wider than that.'

'Supposing you get it? It'll take over our lives. Just for once think about Lucy and me ...' She had played her strongest card.

He stood up, picked up his briefcase and walked out, slamming the door behind him. That afternoon, in a brief statement, Fred Thompson announced that he was putting his name in the ring for the Labour leadership. He told himself that it was what Harry would have wanted.

'What did Elizabeth have to say?' asked Mrs Cook when their paths crossed in the tea room.

'She wasn't keen, but she'll get over it.'

'Listen, Fred,' said Mrs Cook leaning forward and touching his arm, 'whatever you do, don't sacrifice your marriage. It's not worth it. I should know.' Mrs Cook's husband had run off with a French au pair. It made headlines at the time.

'Don't worry, Joan. I won't.' Already part of him hoped that he would lose and that life would return to normal, but deep down he feared the worst.

When he got home the house was dark and empty. There was a note on the kitchen table. It read, 'Gone to my parents'.

* * *

Hustings were held in a committee room dominated by a huge oil painting of Mr Gladstone and his cabinet. In those far-off days, when Britain ruled a third of the world, a mere fourteen members was deemed sufficient. Today, now that our sphere of influence had shrunk somewhat, the cabinet consisted of twenty-two ministers and goodness knows how many juniors. In those days, of course, there had been no secondary education, no pensions, no unemployment pay and no health service to manage.

Just four members of the parliamentary Labour Party had offered themselves up for the poisoned chalice. Beside Thompson the others were Alun Owen Mitchell, a verbose

Welshman who prattled on about Nye Bevan; Felicity Mather, an impressive London barrister who radiated self-confidence; and Albert Stanley Collins a fifty-something northerner who made much of his working-class origins, although, like many of his class, he had adapted with remarkable ease to the perks of office.

Each candidate was given five minutes. They drew lots to decide in which order. The Welshman went first and had barely finished setting out his credentials when he was told, to his evident surprise, that his time was up. Ms Mather set out her stall with admirable clarity, no notes and not a hint of nerves. The gist of Albert Collins' contribution was that the party had had enough of being led by a metropolitan elite and needed to return to its roots. When Thompson's turn came he said, 'We have lost five successive elections, a feat that no principal opposition party has achieved in 200 years. We are in a deep hole and we need to stop digging. That means we are going to have to pay more attention to the concerns of the electorate and abandon some of our cherished shibboleths . . .'

At this, muttering could be heard from certain quarters, not all of them predictable. As far as many of them were concerned, 'listening to the electorate' was code for surrender to the prejudices of the day.

'We are also going to have to rethink our position on the management of migration and relations with the EU.'

On that note he sat down. The tribal banging on tab-letops which usually greeted speeches from the platform was decidedly muted. Jock Steeples, in his usual seat just below the rostrum, did not look happy.

Most of the questions were directed at Thompson. 'Which of our "cherished shibboleths" are we going to abandon?' enquired an overweight Scotsman, one of a cabal who could be found at the same table in the tea room on most sitting days.

Thompson did not prevaricate. 'The one I had in mind was our promise to dispose of Trident. We all know that our possession of nuclear weapons is bonkers. The prob-lem is the Great British Public are rather attached to the British bomb – not that it is all that British, but they don't seem to care. The Tories know it's madness, too. And so too do most of the military, with the exception of the navy. Sooner or later the Tories will get rid of it. We should leave it to them.' This received a mixed reception. Loud applause from the neo-Blairites who, after a long period in the wilderness, were coming back into fashion. Silence from a substantial minority and loud groans from several of the old guard.

'Harry Perkins would be turning in his grave if he could hear you,' shouted one old-timer.

'I'll tell you what would make Harry turn in his grave,' responded Thompson angrily. 'Our refusal to learn

lessons from fifteen years of disaster.' Ignoring an inter-
ruption, he continued. 'Do you think it helps our people
if we remain out of power for ever? Do you think they'll
stick with us for ever? Of course they won't. If we're not
careful some nasty new populist party will emerge from
the ruins. Indeed there are already signs that exactly that
is happening.' He sat down to loud applause. The mood
of the meeting had turned.

'I must confess you had me worried for a minute,' whispered Jock Steeples as the meeting broke up. 'If I were you,
I'd stick to terra firma from now on.'

* * *

Once again Thompson returned to a cold, empty house.
He knew as soon as he opened the door that no one had
been there all day. He lay awake, worrying. Perhaps he
should withdraw and everything would return to normal,
but the loss of face would be considerable. Anyway, with
any luck, after tonight's performance he had blown it.

Fifteen

As it turned out, he hadn't. Not quite, but it was a close run thing. Of the three candidates who made it onto the ballot paper, Thompson received the most nominations, just ahead of Ms Mather. Alun Owen Mitchell, the verbose Welshman, scraped on with just two nominations more than the required minimum. There then followed months of navel gazing as the candidates processed around the country addressing closed meetings of members. At every stop Thompson hammered home his message, 'We've lost *five* successive elections, we can't afford even a little punt on the outcome of a sixth.' It was a message many on the 'no compromise with the electorate' wing of the party didn't wish to hear. On the other hand, as several commentators and not a few members pointed out, their hour had well and truly been and gone. The pendulum was swinging back towards the centre and the centre seemed to mean Ms Mather who had 'Safe Pair of Hands' written all over her in large letters. Also, having only recently been elected, she was unsullied by failures past. Thompson, on the other hand, was a relic of a glorious defeat. Or at least that's how some chose to portray him.

The first ballot was inconclusive. On the second Thompson finished narrowly ahead. He was now the leader of His Majesty's opposition. Acclaim was widespread. As an editorial in *The Times* remarked, Thompson had been in parliament a mere four years and already had substantial achievements under his belt. What's more, unlike just about everyone else on the Labour front bench, he had experience of government.

Only in Thompson's own household was rejoicing decidedly muted. Elizabeth and Lucy had reappeared after an absence of three weeks. Not, as Elizabeth was at pains to make clear, because she had changed her mind, but because Lucy was missing her dad. Thompson did his best to reassure her. He would only do one term and, if he failed, he would resign. Elizabeth's response was uncompromising. 'But supposing you win?' Ah, that was a possibility he had yet to consider in any detail.

In stark contrast to the mood at home, in the world beyond his front door Thompson was a hero, mobbed wherever he went. The novelty would soon wear off – political honeymoons do not last long in this age of the

the media feeding frenzy – and as he soon discovered, there was a downside. Two or three mornings a week they awoke to find cameras on their doorstep, notes pushed through the front door, lenses and microphones poked in their faces. Elizabeth couldn't bear it and she and Lucy soon went back to live with her parents, but it wasn't long before the cameras tracked them down and speculation about the state of their marriage began to appear in the press.

* * *

Meanwhile the economy was going from bad to worse. The symptoms were unmistakable. Long queues of lorries at customs posts. A ballooning trade deficit. A drying up of inward investment. A succession of announcements by British businesses that they would be relocating to the Continent. Regular crises on the border between Northern Ireland and the Republic when the new technology that was supposed to have resolved the customs problem failed to work. The triumphalism that had once surrounded Brexit had long since faded. Assurances from leading Brexiteers that it was just a matter of time, and inviting the public to celebrate the fact that we were no longer a vassal state, gradually gave way to the apportioning of blame. In order of culpability the Brexiteers blamed first the Eurocrats for playing hardball. Then the British government for its half-hearted response. Then the civil service which they accused of foot-dragging and even outright subversion. The mood grew ugly. The Brexit tabloids published lists of traitors which in turn generated hate mail and one or two incidents of violence. Then it all went quiet, and gradually, very gradually, it was apparent that the popular tide was turning.

Looking back it was easy to identify the moment when the scales tipped. It came in the form of a bland little statement from the motor manufacturer, Nissan, that they would be setting up a plant in the Czech Republic to build the latest model of their electric car. For the time being, said the statement, there would be no change to the size of their Sunderland plant, but they could offer no guarantees for the future. Just in case anyone hadn't got the message, the Japanese ambassador gave a series of interviews in which he pointed out that Nissan had come to Sunderland precisely to get inside the EU. They had subsequently been assured by the British government that Brexit would make no difference to their business. Sadly, this had not been the case. Immediately alarm bells began to ring. The Nissan statement was followed by one from Toyota saying only that it was 'reviewing' the future of its British plant. The blame game intensified. It did not go unnoticed that the citizens of Sunderland, many of whom worked at Nissan, had voted overwhelmingly for Brexit. For the first time the polls began to shift. By Year Zero plus five, a clear and growing majority of the Great British Public thought that Brexit had been a mistake. There was even talk of reapplying for EU membership, though there was widespread scepticism among commentators as to whether the UK would any longer be welcome. Not, at any rate, without the consumption of an enormous quantity of humble pie.

On the advice of Mrs Cook, Thompson no longer attended meetings of the Friends. It would, she said, be unwise for the leader of the opposition to appear as if he were the prisoner of a faction. The Friends, however, were well represented on the opposition front bench. With a bit of arm-twisting, he managed to persuade Mrs Cook to return to office as shadow leader of the House. Jock Steeples was, after initial resistance, persuaded to take the foreign affairs portfolio. Ms Mather, whose well-connected friends were already touting her as a future prime minister, was given home affairs and Stephen Carter (who, little known fact, turned out to be fluent in French and German) was given the Europe brief. The post had been abolished in the wake of Brexit but, as Thompson pointed out, Europe hadn't gone away and urgently needed to be engaged with.

The shadow chancellor was Michael Peters, a bright forty-something product of Winchester and St John's

College, Oxford who was rumoured to have made a fortune in the City, but who for some unaccountable reason was also a lifelong Labour Party member. The appointment of Cook and Steeples sparked whingeing from some among the disappointed about old codgers past their sell-by date, but Thompson was unapologetic. In private he referred to Cook and Steeples as 'the adults'. In public they became known as the 'wise men', a label that included Mrs Cook. The appointment that attracted the most comment, however, was none of the above. Sir Matthew Bryant (aka Sir Matt Someone) an erstwhile clandestine member of the Friends and a distinguished former civil servant, had been asked to establish a group of experts to assess the impact of Brexit and to report back within six months. His appointment prompted muttering among the surly Brexiteers about 'mandarins who had sold their country to foreigners', but it was well received by industry and in the City.

* * *

'He's back,' hissed Mrs Jeffries as Thompson arrived for his Friday evening surgery. And sure enough he was. First in line, the unmistakable tattooed, shaven-headed form of Thomas Walter Merton, his sleeves rolled up to his elbows clearly exposing the Union Jack engraved on his right forearm, a nerve twitching in his left temple.

'Well, well, you're a man of influence now.' His tone was insolent. He slouched, legs splayed.

'Not yet. I might be one day, but I have to win an election first.'

'As it happens, that's just what I've come to see you about. What do you say to this?' From his pocket Merton withdrew a tattered press cutting and spread it on the desk between them. The headline, in large bold capitals, read 'BREXIT ALERT'. And beneath, a strapline which read, 'Thompson Plans to Renege on Brexit'.

He offered a cursory glance. 'I wouldn't believe everything you read in the *Daily Mail*.'

'That's why I'm asking you – is it correct?'

'As things stand, Labour has no plans to apply to rejoin the EU.'

'"As things stand" – what's that supposed to mean?'

'It means exactly what I said.'

Suddenly Merton was on his feet. 'You fucking politicians, you're all the fucking same. Can't answer a straight question.' His face was purple. He snatched the cutting from the desk and made for the door, almost colliding with Mrs Jeffries who was hovering there, hand poised over the emergency button.

* * *

'There's a man on the phone. Says he's a friend of Sir Peregrine Craddock's. He's called twice,' said Elizabeth irritably.

It was a Sunday evening. They were staying with Elizabeth's parents in Oxfordshire.

'How did he get this number?'

'Search me.'

'Did he leave a name'?

'Just a number.'

He returned the call.

'Ah, Mr Thompson, so good of you to ring.' The voice was classless. It reminded Thompson of John Major, who still popped up on the radio from time to time.

'My name is Evans, Hugh Evans. I don't think we've met, but the name might ring a bell.' It did indeed; Mr Evans, or rather Sir Hugh, as he would henceforth be known (his name had recently featured in the birthday honours) was the new broom at M15. He was much in the news in these days, now that the secret service no longer bothered to conceal the identity of their top brass. Announcing his appointment, the government spinners, ever anxious to distance themselves from the *ancien régime*, had made much of his having been educated at a comprehensive, although it was Holland Park.

'Peregrine Craddock suggested I give you a call. I gather you've seen him recently.'

'Yes.'

'I don't want to go into detail on the phone, but there are some matters of mutual interest which I would like to discuss . . .'

Thompson said nothing.

' . . . I appreciate you may be sceptical in view of what happened last time round, but much has changed since Perry's day. Indeed he is one of your admirers.'

'Is he now?'

An awkward pause, and then, 'I think we should meet.'

'I will come back to you.'

Thompson replaced the receiver.

'Who was that?' enquired Elizabeth.

'An old friend.'

'Hmmm. Didn't sound like one.' But she didn't press the matter.

* * *

Sir Matthew Bryant's much-anticipated report on the impact of Brexit was launched in the oak-panelled lecture theatre at the Institute of Mechanical Engineers, a stone's throw from the Palace of Westminster. He was flanked by half a dozen captains of industry and commerce, including one who had been prominent in the Brexit campaign, but who had now changed his tune. It was not a lengthy document. One by one it enumerated the arguments advanced by Brexiteers in the run-up to the referendum and its aftermath and then demolished each in the light of experience. The analysis was clinical, avoiding hyperbole and the apportioning of blame. The tone was one of regret rather than anger. The word 'disappointment' featured repeatedly. The conclusion was unequivocal. 'So far as the economy is concerned, with the exception of the fishing industry, Brexit is a disaster. It is not in the national interest to continue down this road.'

'So what are you recommending?' chorused the assembled hacks.

'I do not underestimate the difficulties, but I . . .' He glanced at his colleagues on the platform, several of whom nodded gravely, 'we . . . are firmly of the view that we have no realistic choice but to reapply . . .' At which point his words were drowned. The launch of the report had, it transpired, been infiltrated by a posse of hard-line English nationalists. A punch-up ensued amid cries of treason. Slogans were chanted, microphones wielded, a television camera knocked to the floor and shattered, the flag of St George unfurled. Amid the chaos Sir Matthew and his colleagues slunk from the platform and disappeared through a side door, which was quickly locked. Later, in a series of interviews at an undisclosed location, he repeated his conclusion. In response Number 10 issued a bland little statement saying simply that Brexit was Brexit and there would be no turning back. This prompted a letter, signed by thirty Conservative MPs, urging the prime minister to reconsider. A statement from the leader of the opposition simply thanked Sir Matthew for his report and said the shadow cabinet would consider it in due course. From Brussels there was uncharacteristic silence.

As if to emphasise the sense of gloom and turmoil, the Palace of Westminster was, after years of prevarication, in the process of being vacated to enable the long-delayed renovation to commence. Much of the building was swathed in scaffolding and tarpaulin. For the indefinite future the House of Commons would be meeting under a vast marquee erected in the courtyard of what had once been the Department of Health. Officials had done their best to recreate the atmosphere of the old chamber. The speaker's chair, the mace, the table that separated the two front benches and even the rows of green benches had all been transplanted, but it wasn't the same. Some self-styled modernisers argued that the Palace should be permanently abandoned and converted into a museum, but it took only a few months in the so-called Great Tent to trigger a wave of nostalgia for the old place.

Meanwhile in the Brexit heartlands the mood was growing ugly. Stirred up by the tabloids, angry mobs laid siege to the constituency offices of alleged vacillators.

Homes were picketed, slogans daubed, windows broken, death threats received – often in envelopes enclosing the very newspaper cuttings that had provoked the ire of the righteous. The EU liaison office in Smith Square was the subject of an arson attack, as was the Suffolk cottage of Sir Matthew Bryant, pictures of which had featured in several newspapers, more or less identifying the address. 'Won't this thatch burn nicely,' read a message scrawled across a photograph of the cottage torn from one of our most notorious tabloids. Sir Matthew, now under twenty-four-hour police protection, had been advised to relocate until the fuss died down. Thompson, too, was under growing pressure to state his position. He, after all, had commissioned Sir Matthew's report.

* * *

A shadow cabinet awayday was arranged. In strictest secrecy. A wealthy friend of the shadow chancellor was persuaded to offer the hospitality of his Lutyens mansion in the South Downs. Thompson, Jock Steeples, Mrs Cook and Stephen Carter arrived for dinner the previous evening and the rest were bussed in early next morning from Brighton station. They convened in the library around a long, plain oak table, double doors opening out onto a terrace flanked by two great urns overflowing with petunias. The gardens were by Gertrude Jekyll. Herbaceous borders along each side of a brick path, lined with lavender, and white peonies. 'Nice place you've got here, Fred,' remarked Steeples as they took their seats.

'Don't get too comfortable, Jock. We turn into pumpkins at six p.m.'

Thompson was seated in the centre of the table, his back to the fireplace. Jock Steeples and Michael Peters were opposite, in more or less the positions they would occupy around the cabinet table should the happy day ever dawn when Labour formed a government. Sir Matthew Bryant, still somewhat shell-shocked by the reception his report had received, was seated at Thompson's left hand, a position, which in government would be reserved for the cabinet secretary. The dress code was informal. Only Sir Matthew wore a tie.

'Order.' Thompson banged the table with the flat of his hand. 'First, you have all been asked to leave your mobiles, iPads and any other digital paraphernalia in the safe box in the study. Please confirm that you have done so. If you haven't, please do so now.'

'Oops, sorry.' Tina Morris, the youngest member of the shadow cabinet, said by some to be a rising star, rose from the table and scuttled out of the room, her face flushed.

'Anyone else?'

Silence.

'Good, thank you. Would the general secretary please go to the study and lock the safe?' The general secretary, a smooth young man recently recruited from a Westminster think tank, rose and disappeared through a side door.

'Your gadgets will be returned when we depart, and not until.'

Ignoring the murmurings of dissent, the gist of which was that they were being treated like schoolchildren, Thompson continued. 'Next, I want to thank Sir Matthew for his valuable report which has had the great merit of focusing the minds of the British public on the disaster that is Brexit.' This prompted murmurs of approval from most, but not quite all, of those assembled. This was accompanied by a bout of table banging, the peculiar ritual by which our elected representatives customarily indicate their approbation. Sir Matthew glanced along the table, benignly nodding. After a lifetime in the shadows, he suddenly found himself exposed to the harsh world of front-line politics and, as he didn't mind admitting, he was not at all comfortable. His wife, Lady Emily, was still less enthused. Still, there were worse fates. The fire at their Suffolk cottage had done mercifully little damage, thanks to the vigilance of a neighbour, and they had spent the last three weeks staying with friends in Gascony, waiting for the furore to die down. As a result he was none the worse for wear. On the contrary, he was looking fit and tanned.

'As we all know,' Thompson continued, 'the country remains deeply divided over Brexit, although my instinct is that the tide is turning. I have brought us together today to decide a way forward for our party and for the country. We can either continue to drift with the status quo, in which case we will have to accept a long slow decline into insularity and irrelevance. Or we can be bold . . .' *Bold*, a word that in other contexts meant positively foolhardy. He paused to survey his colleagues. One or two shifted uneasily in their seats, but there was no sign of panic. '. . . and attempt to put the genie back in the bottle.'

'Meaning . . .?' The intervention came from Charlie Forbes, a big, gruff Yorkshireman, whose constituents had voted Leave by a margin of two to one.

'Hang on a minute, Charlie. Let me finish.

'My view is that, if we are to stand any chance of forming a government, we have to go into the next election with an economic programme entirely distinct from that of the current management. We all know that Brexit is a disaster. An increasing number of our voters are waking up to that reality. The issue can no longer be fudged. A handful of zealots have manoeuvred our country into this position and it is time we stood up to them.'

'So what exactly are you proposing?' It was Charlie Forbes again.

'I am proposing that we sound out the EU with a

view to discovering on what terms they would allow us to rejoin.'

Sharp intakes of breath all round. Save for those already in the know.

'Reapply . . .? You must be bloody mad.'

'What's more, since there isn't the slightest chance of today's deliberations remaining confidential for more than a few hours – indeed I'm surprised we've got this far – I'm proposing that we arrive at a clear decision today and announce it to the world before we depart this evening. For that reason I have invited Celia Monaghan, the party's head of communications, to join us here at 5 p.m.'

* * *

They went round the table. A long debate followed. Only Charlie Forbes offered outright opposition, repeatedly citing the views of his constituents until someone responded, 'It's not about your constituents, Charlie, it's about the national interest.' Others talked practicalities: 'Supposing the EU tells us to f-off?' 'What if they continue to insist on open borders?' 'How do we counter arguments about the will of the people?' 'If not now, when?' The only surprise was Felicity Mather. All she said was that it was worth a try, but the risks shouldn't be underestimated.

'Our bright, young, upwardly mobile shadow home secretary's contribution was decidedly muted this morning, for one so obviously a member of the metropolitan elite,' whispered Mrs Cook to Jock Steeples when they adjourned for lunch in the orangery.

'Known in the trade as "doing a Theresa May",' replied Steeples in between mouthfuls of cheese and pickle sandwich. 'She'll be quietly in favour of the new policy until it goes belly-up and, if it does, she will turn. Fred needs to watch out. Poor chap's only been in the job three months and already she's on manoeuvres.'

When they resumed after lunch Thompson responded to the points raised in the morning session. 'If the EU tells us to eff off, we will have to accept that, but my feeling is they won't. Their position is not as strong as it once was. The eastern Europeans are becoming steadily more authoritarian and they are dragging the entire continent with them. The Italians are looking shakier by the day. The migration crisis is unresolved. The Eurocrats need all the help they can get.'

'And so do we,' Mrs Cook chipped in, just loudly enough to be audible around the table.

'As regards open borders, we have to recognise that is the single biggest issue for the British public and it will need to be addressed. My aim will be to persuade Brussels to give us all or part of the moratorium on free movement to which we were entitled after the Eastern bloc signed up in 2004 and which we—'

'*We?* You mean Tony Blair?' a voice at the end of the table interjected.

'Yes, I mean Tony Blair . . . unwisely declined.'

'And if they don't?' It was Charlie Forbes again.

'That's a bridge we will cross when we come to it.'

He paused to fill his glass from a water jug in the centre of the table. 'Mind you don't spill it,' said Stephen Carter, 'or we won't be invited again.'

'As regards arguments about the so-called will of the people,' Thompson took a sip of his water, 'we must respond that it is almost a decade since that accursed – but please don't use that word – referendum. A great deal of water has flowed under the bridge since then and perhaps the time has come for a further test of public opinion. If, after sounding out the EU Commission, we judge that they would respond favourably to an application for renewed British membership, we shall make it a central plank of our election manifesto. So, no one will be able to argue that they haven't been warned. Is everybody happy?'

They went around the table again. Unsurprisingly everyone was not happy. The expression 'high-risk strategy' featured several times in the ensuing discussion. Charlie Forbes talked of having to consider his position. Ms Mather made another brief and bland contribution.

Somebody mischievously enquired what Harry Perkins would have said (it was well known that he had been a Eurosceptic), to which Thompson interjected that Harry was also fearless and no stranger to big and bold strategies.

'Aye, and look where that got us.' It was Charlie Forbes again.

They adjourned for coffee while a short statement was drafted. The text was put to the meeting, there was a bit of haggling – a reference to the need to protect the interests of the fishing industry was inserted along with several minor amendments – but in the end everyone signed up except Charlie Forbes who was still muttering about considering his position. The statement began: 'The shadow cabinet has authorised the leader of the opposition to open discussions with representatives of the EU Commission as to the terms on which Britain might renegotiate its relations with the EU with a view, in the short term, to rejoining the customs union and the single market. In the longer term we do not rule out reapplying for full membership.'

'In other words,' remarked Mrs Cook, as the coach whisked them back to Brighton railway station, 'it's shit or bust.'

Sixteen

The news burst like a bombshell on the political world. The newspapers and the commentators divided along more or less predictable lines. 'At last, a politician prepared to lead,' said the *Financial Times*. 'Harry's Boy Launches Brexit Exocet' was the *Mirror*'s take. *The Times* opted for studious neutrality. 'FRED THE SHRED' was the *Sun*'s headline, a reference to a late, unlamented banker, one of the architects of the 2008 financial crash. Even so, there were those who noted that the *Sun*'s reporting of this latest twist in the Brexit soap opera was uncharacteristically restrained. Was some unseen hand at work? The *Telegraph* led on the news that a group of hedge funders, several of whom had made fortunes out of Brexit, were launching yet another campaign to defend Britain's sovereignty. 'No Turning Back' was their slogan. That too rang bells from an earlier era.

As for the rest of the Brexit tabloids, they were beside themselves. In the days that followed they grew steadily more splenetic, urging their readers to new heights of fury, and it was from them that many of the online commentators took their cue.

* * *

An inspector from the Metropolitan Police Protection Command came to check over the flat. 'You can't stay here,' he advised, 'not safe in the current climate.' His name was Nigel. A graduate of the University of Newcastle, in politics and international studies, no less. He wore glasses and carried a copy of the *Guardian*. The first thing he surveyed was the bookshelves. 'Politics today is not like it was when I was a lad,' he remarked wistfully. 'In the sixties the prime minister could walk down Whitehall unmolested. And anyone could walk through Downing Street. Had myself photographed on the front step, I did. Those gates were only supposed to be temporary, but from the moment they went up I knew they'd never come down. First it was the IRA, then the jihadis. Now it's Brexit. Mind you, it comes to something when even the leader of the opposition isn't safe.' He added, 'There's even talk of having to offer protection to the Lib Dem leader. Now that really is a sign of the times.'

His eye alighted on Alan Bullock's biography of Bevin. 'Ernie Bevin, now there's a great man. Don't make 'em like old Ernie anymore. Mind you, I liked that Harry Perkins, too. A friend of yours, wasn't he?'

'I worked for him.'

'Ah yes, so you did. Didn't agree with him on everything, but Harry Perkins was a man of substance. True to his principles. Today's politicians are minnows by comparison.' He paused and added, 'No offence, sir. Maybe you're going to be the exception.'

'I hope so.'

They got down to business. 'As I say, nice flat and all that, but I'm afraid you can't stay here. No way. A security nightmare. Too exposed, no rear exit, nowhere to billet the protection officers.'

'Officers, plural? How many?'

'They'll be a team of eight.'

'Eight?'

'Not all at once. They work in pairs, round the clock.'

'Do I get a say in this?'

'Not really, sir. It's decided in Whitehall, by a committee with access to intelligence. Their assessment is that you are at risk.'

'What do you advise?'

'Well, the Home Office have an apartment in a safe house in Belgravia which they might be prepared to lend you. Nice address. Comfortable. A mews exit. A basement flat for the protection officers.'

Elizabeth, silent until now, said she was having none of it. Fred could go if he wanted, but she and Lucy were staying put.

'I wouldn't advise that, madam. As I said, there's some real loonies around these days. What would you do if someone shoved a fire cracker through the letterbox?'

They agreed to reflect and come back to him in a couple of days. In the meantime, there would be a policeman stationed outside the front door. If nothing else, it would at least help with door-stepping reporters and cameramen who lay in ambush. Each morning when Fred opened the front door he had to force his way through a scrum of insolent journalists, thrusting microphones under his nose and cameras in his face, shouting questions, demanding answers.

'Why are all these people shouting at Daddy?' Lucy enquired one day. 'Is it because Daddy is famous?'

* * *

In the end it was agreed that, for the foreseeable future, Elizabeth and Lucy would live with her parents. Lucy would have to change schools, but there was nothing they could do about that. 'There's a good prep school nearby. My father has offered to pay.'

'For goodness' sake, please don't, Lizzie. That'll bring down another great shower of shite on our heads. There's no shortage of good state schools in and around Oxford.'

There was a row, but in the end she gave in. 'Another little nail in the coffin of our marriage,' he thought, but did not say.

'Oh, Fred, what have you got us into?' she sighed.

* * *

Nigel from Protection was duly informed. 'A wise decision, if you don't mind my saying so, sir. And, of course, there is an upside, quite apart from the flat in Belgravia.'

'Oh?'

'It comes with a bombproof Jag and a driver, courtesy of HMG. A perk of office, you could say, sir. You'd be surprised how reluctant some of your colleagues are when the time comes to part with it, as you will do one day.'

'I shall be only too glad.'

'That's what they all say, sir. To begin with.'

* * *

Thompson commenced a tour of European capitals. He was careful to emphasise that he was not offering a surrender. There would have to be concessions from the

Europeans too. David Cameron had come home with nothing and look what happened. That was a fate he was determined to avoid. What he wanted was a credible proposition. One that he could put to the electorate in a general election. One that addressed their concerns, in particular on migration. He would only get one chance and this was it. The French were haughty. The Germans non-committal. The Swedes, the Danes and the Dutch sceptical, but open to discussion. The Italians, Austrians and just about all the former Eastern bloc had continued to drift right, and far-right parties were making gains in France, Germany, Spain and the Netherlands. Increasingly there was alarmist talk of a return to the 1930s.

In private Thompson was robust. 'How can you afford to be so complacent?' he demanded of the French president, who was particularly insufferable. 'You must know where this path leads. Look what is happening. Your precious project is crumbling before your eyes. You need us and we need you.' To the cautious Germans he said, 'I am taking a big risk. All I am asking in return is that you take a small one and climb down from your high horse before it is too late.'

At home he walked a fine line. Cartoons in the Brexit press depicting him as a dwarf going cap in hand to arrogant giants. Editorials talked of a choice between freedom and national humiliation. The *Sun* launched a 'Fly the Flag for Britain' campaign which was quickly adopted by other tabloids and spread like wildfire through housing estates which had once been Labour strongholds.

Nerves began to fray. 'I hope you know what you are doing, Fred,' whispered Ronnie Morgan, one of his staunchest supporters, 'you should hear what they are saying about you down at the club.' There was grumbling, too, at the monthly meeting of his constituency management committee and on the party's national executive. In the polls the party continued to lag behind the incumbents, although the gap had closed marginally. The polls also indicated a revival of support for the far-right English Nationalist Party who were becoming increasingly brazen. Several of Thompson's shadow cabinet colleagues were noticeably silent and one or two were reported to be privately critical. Twice his minders had intervened to rescue him from angry mobs. An attempt to hold a series of public rallies had to be called off on police advice. On one occasion Thompson was sprayed with red paint, on another he was hit by eggs. And the threats multiplied. Directed not only at Thompson, but also against Elizabeth and Lucy. Mrs Jeffries, in his Sheffield office, who was also the target for much of the abuse, was saying she didn't think she could cope much longer. In public Thompson was unwavering. Privately he began to wonder if he had bitten off more than he could chew. And then, gradually, imperceptibly at first, things started to change.

* * *

The meeting with Sir Hugh Evans took some time to arrange. Thompson resisted a suggestion that he come to M15 headquarters on Millbank and turned down Sir Hugh's offer of dinner in a private room at his club. In the end they settled for beer and Waitrose sandwiches at Thompson's temporary abode in Belgravia. In the best traditions of his profession, Sir Hugh entered via the mews entrance and was shown up the servants' staircase. There was some small talk first, Sir Hugh enquiring after Elizabeth and Lucy as though they were old friends, wondering how they were coping with what he called 'all this fuss' and affecting to admire the Hogarth prints from the government art collection on the sitting room wall. And then to business.

'We think we can help you,' he said.

'Really? I thought you guys had given up interfering in politics.'

'We have. We can't take sides, of course.'

'Of course,' allowing just a ghost of a smile to cross his face.

'No, seriously, it's different now. There was a big clear-out after that unfortunate business with Perkins.'

'So I should hope.'

'Talking of which, Sir Peregrine sends his regards, by the way. Actually this meeting was his idea.'

Thompson was struck by how normal he seemed. Marks & Spencer rather than Fortnum & Mason. Shepherd's Bush rather than St James's. Almost youthful in appearance. A certain boyish charm. A full head of hair, greying at the temples. Self-made, the product of a provincial university. A slight air of diffidence, lacking the armour-plated self-confidence of those educated at the better public schools.

The room, for all its fading elegance, gave the impression of being camped in rather than lived in. A briefcase unopened on a table by the window, bookshelves empty save for a couple of Chinese vases and volume three of Charles Moore's monumental biography of Thatcher, left by a previous occupant. 'It's safeguarding national interest we are concerned with.'

'That's what they said last time.'

Sir Hugh ignored the barb and sailed smoothly on. 'What is of particular concern to us is the security co-operation with our friends on the Continent.'

'I thought that, at least, was settled.'

'In theory, yes. In practice, no. We no longer enjoy the degree of co-operation that we were used to and as a result a number of terrorist suspects have slipped through the net. In fact we had a close shave only the other day. Can't go into details, but it set alarm bells ringing, that I can tell you.'

The light was fading, Thompson reached for the lamp.

'There's another problem, too. We've fallen out with our so-called "brothers" at Vauxhall Cross. Relations have never recovered from all that post-9/11 torture business. They've lied, wriggled and obfuscated, but they were found out in the end. Millions of pounds have had to be paid to victims, some of them not particularly savoury individuals, in order to buy silence. We suspect that some of that money has found its way into terrorist networks. One of my predecessors was so furious when she found out what they'd been up to that she chucked their liaison officers out of Millbank and cut off relations with them. We've done our best to patch things up, but the damage has never really been repaired. In a nutshell that's why we urgently need to re-establish full co-operation with our European counterparts.'

'What's this got to with me?' A fly settled on his forehead and he waved it away.

'It may surprise you to know that you have a lot of admirers in the Service.'

'It does surprise me.'

'Seriously, there is enormous admiration for the stand you have taken. Plus we all know it's not in Britain's economic interests to go it alone. That's becoming clearer with every day that passes.'

* * *

A tap on the door. The housekeeper with a flask of coffee and two mugs. 'Sorry to interrupt, sir, but I'll be knocking off soon and I thought you might like this.' She was a large, florid, homely woman, whose accent suggested she came from somewhere up north.

'Thank you, Mrs Parker. Just leave it on the table.'

'The real stuff, sir. Bought the beans this morning, so I did. From that Italian shop, the one I was telling you about. In Soho. Would you like me to pour?'

'Just leave the flask on the table, please. I'll deal with it.'

'Milk and sugar on the table, spoons in the drawer.'

'Thank you.'

'Oh, and mind you use the mat. Don't want any rings on the table, do we now?'

She closed the door behind her.

Sir Hugh smiled benignly. 'Presumably she's been vetted.'

'I assume so. One of yours, I shouldn't be surprised. Her husband is a policeman.'

* * *

An interlude while Thompson poured the coffee and searched out the spoons. And then, 'You were saying?'

'I was saying that we may be able to help you.'

'I'd rather you didn't.'

'Hear me out.'

'I'm all ears.'

'There is about to be a development which we believe may have a major political impact. The *Sun* is about to come out for you.' He paused to let this news sink in. The silence was broken by the sound of a passing ambulance siren.

A sharp intake of breath and then, 'You've got to be kidding.'

'No. I am deadly serious. For some months, since old man Murdoch passed on, we've been talking to the younger Murdochs. They are somewhat more liberal than their father, you won't be surprised to hear. What's more, unlike their father, they aren't interested in messing about in British politics and they don't have strong opinions about the EU. In fact one of them is positively in favour, so to some extent we are pushing at an open door. Their main concern is that, in the short term at least, there will be a backlash from their readers who are heavily nationalist, though there are signs that a little light has come on in some quarters. The recent Nissan announcement was a wake-up call if ever there was one.' Sir Hugh paused and then said quietly, 'They do want something in return, however.'

'Ah. So I have to sell my soul, do I?'

A mirthless grin and then Sir Hugh said quickly. 'The Murdochs want an assurance that you will not break up their UK empire or enquire too deeply into their tax arrangements.'

'And, if I don't give it?'

'Then all bets are off, I'm afraid.'

* * *

What followed is highly classified. Sir Hugh made no note of the meeting and Thompson breathed not a word, even to his closest confidants. All that is known is that ten days later the headquarters of News Corp in New York announced that there was to be a major shake-up in the management of their British assets. The chief executive, a man who had spent thirty years in the service of the Murdoch dynasty, would be leaving forthwith with a substantial retirement package and a glowing tribute to his many years of loyal service. The brash young editor of the *Sun* would be departing for Sydney, Australia, where he had been offered an unspecified role in the management of the empire's Antipodean assets. His two deputies would also be leaving with immediate effect. Finally, the editor of the *Sunday Times* would be leaving for a management position in New York, his move cushioned by a substantial relocation package. Most remarked upon, however – indeed, it was greeted with astonishment – was the name of the new chief executive: a former senior civil servant, author of a recent controversial report into the impact of Brexit who was said to be a close confidant of the leader of His Majesty's opposition. Sir Matthew Bryant, no less.

Seventeen

The general election came sooner than anyone had anticipated. In these uncertain times the days of four- and five-year parliaments were long gone. For a while the government, its majority eroded by a series of by-election defeats, had been limping on, once again propped up by Ulster Unionists. Indeed, with each new crisis, the public was becoming accustomed to the sight of grim-faced Unionists marching up Downing Street to present a new list of demands to the beleaguered prime minister until finally ministers wearied of the whole business and pulled stumps.

The change in the editorial line of the *Sun* came about slowly. The tone of its reporting was notably more reasonable; gone were the accusations of treachery and betrayal which had been a regular feature of its reporting under the previous management. Gradually, almost imperceptibly,

Sun readers were being weaned off Brexit and fed instead with more traditional fare, the antics of errant soap stars and Premier League footballers. Migration scares, which had long been a prominent feature of *Sun* news coverage, disappeared. Increasingly the paper focused on the downside of Brexit, the construction of the new Nissan plant in the Czech Republic, the queue of lorries at Dover and other British ports following the breakdown of the new customs technology, and the growing shortage of key workers in the NHS. The *Sunday Times*, meanwhile, ran feature articles on those it dubbed the 'Brexit Billionaires' who were moving their assets offshore to escape the consequences of the calamity they had helped bring about. It was, remarked Mrs Cook at a meeting of the shadow cabinet, as if someone had flicked a switch. Thompson just smiled and said nothing.

His stock, meanwhile, was rising. He was judged to have done well in the televised party leaders' debate, which attracted viewing figures on a par with the royal wedding and the World Cup. Favourable profiles appeared in the Murdoch press and on Sky Television. His association with the late Harry Perkins was no longer the liability it had once been. On the contrary, Harry was often referred to in glowing terms. In death he had achieved the status of a national treasure, something he had signally failed to do in life. Thompson, however, was at pains to emphasise that he was his own man. He even made overtures to Brexit voters, taking care to distinguish between ordinary people and what he called the handful of Brexit zealots who had taken the British people on a ride to nowhere. They had been right, he said, to be concerned about migration. An annual population increase of 250,000 a year *was* unsustainable and must be addressed. A moratorium on free movement from eastern Europe would be a condition of any renegotiation with the EU. As for asylum seekers, while our door would remain open to those genuinely fleeing persecution, his government would clamp down hard on the rackets, and those who did not qualify would be returned to their countries of origin.

None of this could change the fact that Britain remained a deeply divided country. The traditional, class-based fault lines were rapidly eroding. What mattered now was where you stood on Brexit. You were either for or against. There was no middle ground. The result was that Thompson and his party polled surprisingly well in parts of the Home Counties that had not returned Labour candidates for decades while, by contrast, disaffection ran high in what were once Labour's northern strongholds. The departure of the *Sun* from the field of battle had little impact on the flow of bile that dominated the digital media, and the remaining Brexit tabloids continued to generate fear and loathing. Threats of murder and rape continued to clog the inboxes and Twitter feeds of politicians, Labour and Conservative, perceived to have strayed from the one true path.

Publication of the Labour manifesto with its promise to reopen negotiations with the EU only provoked greater paroxysms of fury. 'TRAITOR' screamed the Brexit tabloids over a grim-looking picture of Thompson, head down as he ran the media gauntlet between his front door and his armoured Jaguar. Posters bearing his photograph and headed 'Wanted for Treason' began to circulate in the pubs and clubs of Brexit strongholds. He was now accompanied everywhere by not two, but four protection officers, three in a backup Range Rover. On police advice his schedule of public meetings was drastically trimmed and those attending had to pass through metal detectors. His Sheffield office was closed and relocated to a third-floor office block with telephone entry and security cameras. From all over the country came reports of candidates faced with threats and intimidation. Half a dozen arrests were made, one of them of a man who had tried to force his way into a candidate's office carrying a machete. Brexit, remarked one commentator, had brought out the worst in the British people. 'It seems to have given permission to every little bedsit extremist to say out loud that which he previously only dared say in the privacy of his own four walls.'

* * *

As for Elizabeth, she was conspicuous by her absence. By mutual agreement she would remain in seclusion at her parents' home until election night when she had magnanimously agreed to appear alongside her husband at the count.

Eighteen

As usual, Sunderland South was the first seat to declare and, despite earlier misgivings, the Labour vote held up well, although to the dismay of some observers the English Nationalist candidate polled more than 3,000 votes. In Torquay the Conservative candidate, a hard-line Brexiteer, regained the seat from the Liberal Democrats and promptly treated the nation to a bloodcurdling prediction of the social breakdown that he confidently anticipated in the event of a Labour victory. The first results from the Home Counties were generally good, with Labour picking up seats they had not held for twenty years in places like Hastings, Harwich and Dartford. The Lib Dems recaptured Richmond. Sheffield Hallam returned to Labour, along with several Tory-held marginals in the West Midlands. The shock announcement two days previously by the director general of the CBI that he and his fellow council members were, for the first time ever, advising a vote for Labour was thought to have carried particular weight in the industrial heartlands, but the *Sun*'s declaration earlier in the week that 'WE'RE BACKING HARRY'S BOY' was generally thought to be the turning point of the campaign.

In Sheffield, Thompson and Elizabeth watched events unfold from the comfort of the mayor's parlour in the company of Vera Clarke, and a handful of local loyalists. Lucy, in her best dress adorned with a red rosette, had fallen asleep on a sofa. Elizabeth had tried to persuade her to stay home with Granny and Grandpa, but Lucy had insisted. 'I want to see Daddy become prime minister,' she said. 'I told everyone at school that my daddy is going to be famous.' A uniformed police officer was on guard outside the door. On the television a noticeably aged David Dimbleby was predicting a substantial Labour majority. 'A seminal moment in British politics,' he remarked, 'the Brexit tide has turned. From outside, the cheers of the crowd were just audible in the inner sanctum, growing louder with each new result.

Thompson's phone began to vibrate. It didn't ring often. Only a dozen members of his inner circle had the number. It was Jock Steeples, who had just been returned with a record majority, 'Well, son, you've done it. Congratulations.'

'A bit early yet, Jock. The night is young.'

'Bullshit, son. You've won. You're going to be prime

minister. I hope you know what you've let yourself in for.'
He rang off, chuckling.

'Oh, Fred,' said Elizabeth. She kissed him lightly on the
cheek. The first spontaneous sign of affection in months.

'Is Daddy prime minister yet?' It was Lucy calling from
the couch.

'Not yet, darling.'

One of the minders put his head round the door. 'You're
wanted in the council chamber, sir.'

* * *

In recent years the counting of votes for the six or seven
parliamentary seats in and around Sheffield had taken
place in the antiseptic surroundings of the English
Institute of Sport, a vast concoction of concrete and steel,
which, although ideal for turning out Olympic champi-
ons, imposes a somewhat deadening atmosphere on the
excitement surrounding a general election. Thompson
was therefore relieved when, for security reasons, his
minders insisted that his result and his alone should be
declared in the more sedate surroundings of Sheffield's
Victorian Town Hall, the very place that a generation ago
had witnessed the rise of his old mentor, Harry Perkins.

Accompanied by Elizabeth and a by now wide-awake
Lucy, two vigilant minders, the redoubtable Vera Clarke

and his much put-upon constituency secretary, Mrs Jeffries, his passage illuminated by television arc lights, Thompson made his way slowly along the marble corridor to the anteroom, noting as he did so the epigram carved above the door, 'Be Ye Wise as Serpents and Harmless as Doves'.

'St Matthew's Gospel,' whispered one of the loyalists, a Sunday school teacher. He added with a smirk, 'The bit that comes before is more relevant in our case, "I send you forth as a sheep among wolves ..."'

Outside, the baying of the crowd grew louder. 'WE WANT FRED, WE WANT FRED.'

'They're calling your name, Daddy,' said Lucy, her face aglow.

They passed into the council chamber. A space designed to impress. A relic of the days when councillors enjoyed power and status, when they had money to spend, patronage to dispense. Nowadays it was all cuts, cuts, cuts. The glory days had long gone. Only the trappings remained.

The councillors' desks had been reorganised into a semicircle around which tellers sat idly, trays empty, chatting, their work done. All that remained was to sit back, soak up the atmosphere and await the result. To one side a stack of now redundant ballot boxes. On a table in the centre, ballot papers neatly bundled into batches of 100, in trays labelled with the names of each candidate. A glance was sufficient to confirm the outcome. Only the size of Thompson's majority remained to be announced.

As he entered the hubbub faded. A ripple of applause. In the gallery, a wall of cameras recording his every step as he strode confidently towards the dais where the returning officer and the other candidates were already assembled. Elizabeth, Lucy and the rest of the little party now fell behind. He walked alone, all eyes on him. The screen above the platform, streaming results from around the country, switched live to Sheffield Parkside, cameras briefly scanning the faces of the expectant crowd outside and then back into the council chamber as Thompson mounted the stage.

He paused to shake hands with each of the other candidates: a motley lot, each anxious to claim their fifteen seconds of fame. Only the English Nationalist, fresh from a recent court appearance, refused Thompson's proffered hand. Ordinarily the declaration of an election result in a safe seat such as this would be of no great interest, but by now everyone present knew that they were on the eve of a great event. A moment that would be remembered for years to come.

Below the stage, corralled behind a rope barrier, 200 heavily vetted election observers – each party had their quota. The English Nationalists, sharp-suited, shaven headed, red, white and blue rosettes, standing slightly apart from the rest. Among the Labour supporters, little Lucy, her face shining, stood clutching her mother's hand. She waved at her dad and he winked back at her.

A distinguished-looking man, with a good head of grey hair and gold-rimmed spectacles perched on the end of his nose, stepped up to the lectern. The crowd fell silent. He made a little show of adjusting his spectacles. This was his big moment. The eyes of the nation were upon him. The words rolled slowly from his tongue. 'I ... Peter James Baldwin ... returning officer for the constituency of Sheffield Parkside ... hereby give notice that the number of votes cast is as follows:

'Jonathan Algernon Crispin Blagdon, The Green Party'.

At the mention of his name a pleasant-looking, rosy-cheeked young man in a tweed jacket and corduroy trousers raised both hands to be greeted with a mixture of polite applause and, from the uncouth, mild sniggering at the mention of the candidate's middle names. 'Not from round these parts,' someone said in a loud stage whisper.

'743 votes.'

'Michael Francis Bonham Carter, Liberal Democrat ... 2,120.'

Cue ironic cheers from some quarters matched by frantic cheering from a handful of the assembled. There were not a lot of Liberal Democrats in Parkside.

'Richard Francis Dixon, Anti-Fascist Alliance ... 980.'

Another ripple of applause in which some Labour supporters joined, drowned out by the jeers of the English Nationalists.

The returning officer raised his hand for silence.

'Melissa Catherine Farrow, Conservative candidate ...' The camera focused briefly on smart young woman in a blue trouser suit, blond hair swept back in an Alice band.

'... 4,780.'

Polite applause and a few 'hear-hears' from a posse of well-dressed pensioners and a couple of posh-looking youths in open-necked shirts. Despite a heroic effort to pretend otherwise, Melissa, an investment analyst, was a fish out of water in Sheffield. Tomorrow she would be going home to the more comfortable climes of West Sussex and would not be returning.

'Frank Oswald Lawton, English Nationalist Party ... 3,941.'

Cue loud cheering from the English Nationalists, accompanied by much booing and hissing from the rest of the crowd, all except the small band of Tories who stood in awkward silence. One of the Anti-Fascists was caught on camera making a discreet V-sign in the direction of the Nationalists.

'Tracey Jane Norton, Monster Raving Loony Party ...'

All eyes briefly turned to a young woman with green

hair, a ring through her lips and tattoos on various parts of her anatomy.

'... 98 votes.'

Another pause for the hubbub to die down, and then, 'Frederick Aneurin' (yes, that was his middle name, once a source of embarrassment, now an electoral asset) 'Thompson, the Labour candidate ... 28,000 ...'

The hall erupted, many of the tellers joining in, little Lucy beside herself, applauding, leaping up and down. Outside, the dull roar of the crowd.

Twice the returning officer had to call for order before he could make himself heard, '... 28,956.' More cheers. 'I, therefore, declare Frederick Aneurin Thompson duly elected as the member of parliament for Sheffield Parkside.'

Thompson stepped up to the microphone. He thanked everybody who needed to be thanked and then addressed the nation, his every sentence interrupted by cheers. 'It is absolutely clear from this result, and from results elsewhere in the country, that by tomorrow morning we shall be in a position to form a government. This marks a sea change in British politics. This is the moment when the British people have decided to reject the follies of the past and move forward to a brighter future. We shall do so in a spirit of tolerance and goodwill. Once again Britain shall become an outward-looking country, holding our heads high. It will not be plain sailing. I do not underestimate the difficulties which lie ahead. But to coin a phrase from a previous era, "Things Can Only Get Better".'

And with that he shook hands with the returning officer and stepped smartly down from the stage, into the warm embrace of his wife and daughter, as all around people vied to shake his hand, minders looking on warily.

'Sir.' It was Nigel, from Protection, who had come in person to supervise security arrangements for the big night. He wouldn't have missed this for anything. 'If you don't mind my saying so, I think it would be wise to go back upstairs and wait for things to calm down. Then we can depart for London ... there is a rear entrance. We will bring the car round ...'

'A rear entrance? You must be joking, Nigel. If you think I'm going to skulk out of a back door on this, the biggest night of my life, you've got another think coming. First, I'm going to the front to address a few words to the crowd outside, after that we'll see ...'

'With all due respect, sir ...'

All around people were snapping him on their mobiles, while the minders did their best to keep them at bay.

'WE WANT FRED,' came the roar from outside.

'Nigel, get real. These people want to see me. I can't just slink out the back. We're going out.'

With that Thompson began to stride towards the double doors that led through the anteroom to the grand staircase. Lucy clutching his hand on one side, Elizabeth on the other. Well-wishers slapping him on the back, mobiles aloft, Nigel and his team warily clearing a path, people still applauding.

'WE WANT FRED.' The chants grew louder. Uniformed policemen were holding the doors open. A scrum around them now; the minders grim-faced, not quite in control.

A hand emerged from the melee, on his right side. At first Thompson took it to be a well-wisher, wanting to shake his hand. He let go of Elizabeth ... Too late, he glimpsed the Union Jack tattoo ... protruding from under a long-sleeved shirt.

* * *

He never even saw the blade. No one did, until it was too late. Or even felt anything as it entered the soft flesh below his ribcage. Once, twice ... three times. The minders were a full two paces ahead, eyes elsewhere. Elizabeth screamed. Behind, he was dimly aware of a scuffle and a loud voice bawling, 'BRITAIN FIRST ... DEATH TO TRAITORS.' The minders swung round, surprised.

The crowd around him had melted. Except for Lucy, who was still clutching his left hand. For a few seconds they stood completely alone. Somewhere to his right someone was screaming. It sounded like Elizabeth, but he couldn't be sure. The cheers and applause had stopped. It was very quiet. Something had happened, but he wasn't sure what.

And then, suddenly, a sharp pain in his right side; he clutched at his shirt, something warm and wet trickled over his fingers, a red stain spreading. 'BRITAIN FIRST,' the voice, more distant now, was still calling as he toppled slowly backwards, a tree in the forest falling.

His eyes were still open. Lucy was hugging him. 'My dad, my dad!' she was screaming. Someone pulled her off. Faces peered down at him. Then Elizabeth was on her knees beside him. 'Fred, Fred, Fred,' was all she said.

'Sorry, Lizzie . . .' Quietly. Almost inaudible. She put her ear to his mouth, '. . . so, so sorry.'

He closed his eyes. Darkness. And then, 'Hello, Dad.'

'Who's that?'

'It's me, Dad. Don't you remember?'

A smiling little face. Radiant. No sign of Malfoy. Her golden curls had come back. It was Little Sunshine.

'See you again soon, Dad. On our island.'

And then she, too, was gone and the darkness returned.

* * *

Later, all in good time, there would be a judicial inquiry. One question above all dominated. How, in the name of all that is holy, had Thomas Walter Merton managed to penetrate the wall of security around the election count? He was, it transpired, an election observer. Not, as one might have expected, for the English Nationalists. On the contrary, security footage of the count showed that he steered well clear of them. No, he had been there as a volunteer with the Green Party. But surely he had been vetted? Yes indeed he had, like everyone else admitted to Town Hall on that fateful night, but it turned out he had another identity, complete with driving licence, passport, bank account. All in the name of Joseph Michael Fortune, a forklift truck driver in an out-of-town warehouse who shared the same lodgings as Merton and was a member of the Green Party. Apparently Merton had been out campaigning with the Greens. Fellow campaigners spoke well of him. He had worked hard, leafleting, door knocking. He had changed his appearance, too. Positively respectable, he looked. Regrown his hair, always wore long sleeves, no sign of tattoos. How, then, had he managed to smuggle a six-inch blade into the Town Hall, past not one but two metal detectors? Turned out he had brought it in three days earlier and hidden it in the cistern of the gents' toilet. CCTV footage taken during the count showed him disappearing in the direction of the toilets fifteen minutes before the result was announced. As for the real Joseph Michael Fortune, his remains were discovered a month after the election in a peat bog on the moors above Kinder Scout.

* * *

The funeral procession set off from Barker's Pool. Like his mentor, Harry Perkins, Thompson's coffin lay for three days in state in the City Hall to allow the public to pay their respects. They came in large numbers. Flowers piled up on the steps, many with messages attached. 'So long, Fred. You were our last hope,' said one. The crowds that lined the route were every bit as large as those who had turned out for Harry. This time, however, there was no last-minute appearance by the king. He had, however, publicly spoken of his dismay at what had happened and Elizabeth received a long letter of condolence, hand-delivered from Clarence House (still his official residence), regretting that he had not had the chance to get to know Fred, for whom he expressed much admiration, and full of angst about what was happening to the country.

There was a big turnout from parliament, headed by the speaker and the leaders of all parties. Felicity Mather had been appointed Labour's acting prime minister and it was widely expected that in due course she would be chosen to replace Fred Thompson. As before, Jock Steeples and Mrs Cook were in the front rank of the mourners, along with Stephen Carter, who was for the time being at least, the Foreign Office minister in charge of relations with Europe.

The wicker coffin was topped by a wreath of white lilies and little posy of flowers, to which was attached a note in large, childish handwriting: 'TO MY DEAREST, DEAREST DADDY, WITH LOVE FROM LUCY XXXXXXXXXXXXXXX'. To which she had added a postscript: 'I hope you like these flowers. They came from Granny and Grandpa's garden.'

Immediately behind the hearse, a bewildered little girl in her best white dress to which was pinned a single red rose, face stained with tears, clutching her mother's hand. Elizabeth, ashen-faced, in a dark two-piece suit, a red rose in her buttonhole, staring resolutely ahead, expressionless. Alongside, her parents. Mother upright, sprightly, stoic. Father, ruddy-cheeked, ram-rod straight, white handker-chief protruding from his breast pocket, limping slightly, supporting himself with a gold-topped walking stick. Behind them the lord mayor, resplendent in his gold chain and robes of office.

Among the wreaths, displayed on the steps of the City Hall, one from an address in Somerset, labelled in an illegible scrawl. Another, the source of much speculation, was signed simply, 'Hugh'.

The city fathers had wanted to bury Fred Thompson in the General Cemetery, alongside the city's other favourite son, but Elizabeth would have none of it. Instead, following a short, private service, his remains were cremated. In due course she and Lucy would travel to 'their' island where the ashes would be scattered along with those of their beloved Catherine, on the grassy mound above the beach and the little white cottage in which they had once lived so happily. A small cairn marks the spot.

* * *

Meanwhile, in the Taiwan Straits, it was reported that the USS *Donald Trump* had been in collision with a Chinese warship.

THE LORD CARDINAL

The Story of a Man Whose Greatest Achievement
Occurred after His One Hundredth Birthday

On the morning of his one hundredth birthday the Lord Cardinal rose, as always, before dawn. Perched upon the edge of his bed he dressed himself, arthritic fingers trembling over each of the buttons on his soutane. Then, taking up his walking frame, he shuffled along the corridor to the chapel, where Father Anselm and the sisters were waiting to say mass.

He took a light breakfast in the Oriel Room, in his favourite armchair by the window, with views across verdant lawns to the distant ocean. Pedro, the gardener, was already pottering among the rose beds. After breakfast he skimmed the morning papers, his portrait dominating the front pages. *El Mercurio* carried a special supplement, celebrating his long life, and a lengthy editorial singing his praises while tactfully omitting any mention of his various run-ins with the regime. At the bottom of an inside page, news of the civil war that had spluttered intermittently for more than two decades. Rebels, or *Los Banditos* as the local media preferred to call them, were reported to have attacked the police station in a hamlet 30 miles from the capital. According to the paper, there was no loss of life, although the police station had been demolished. At one time it had seemed that *Los Banditos* might have threatened the capital itself, but now – thanks to the iron rule of His Excellency the Life President – they were mainly confined to the impoverished south.

At nine, Father Anselm wheeled in a trolley piled high with cards and telegrams, and together they spent an hour leafing through them, the priest drawing his master's attention to those of particular interest. Father Anselm reported that a crowd had been gathering in the piazza since just after daybreak and was now so great that it spilled out into the side streets, where state television had erected screens for the benefit of those who could not get into the square. The crowd were singing hymns and chanting his name. Despite his impaired hearing, the sound was just about audible in the library.

Just before ten, Sister Annunciata appeared, in a state of great agitation, to say that they were to stand by for a call from the Holy Father. The call came ten minutes later.

'Carlo, my dear friend, many, many congratulations. You are the first to reach this milestone. Still in office, after all these years. And in reasonable health, I trust?'

'I cannot complain, Holiness. The Lord has been merciful.'

'Merciful? He positively shines his light upon you.'

'But not, alas, on my poor country, Holiness.'

'Ah no, alas. But were it not for you the situation would be a great deal worse.'

'That is why I have been spared, Holiness.'

'Perhaps, Carlo, but do you not think the time has come for you to take a well-earned rest?' Delicate territory, this. In recent years all conversations with the Holy Father eventually arrived at this point. 'After all, you have done more for the church and for your country than anyone could reasonably expect. And you have exceeded the official retirement age by a quarter of a century. Even Dr Mannix in Melbourne never quite reached his century. You are the all-time record holder.'

'I am not concerned with records, Holiness.' The Lord Cardinal's tone had hardened.

'No, no. Of course. All I meant was . . .'

'I am all that stands between civilisation and a return to barbarism. That is why I have been spared.'

'Quite so, Carlo. You are right, I am sure, but there must be others who could assume your heavy burden.'

'Sadly not, Holiness. Unfortunately, the General listens to no one but me. I must outlive him.'

'Outlive? What age is the General?'

'Seventy-three.'

'But he could last another decade or more.'

'He has not been blessed with the same good health as me. And in any case, who knows? I, too, may survive for another decade.'

The Holy Father did not persist. Sooner or later the issue would have to be confronted, or perhaps divine intervention would settle the matter, but not today. He changed the subject. They had been acquainted for many years. Ever since the Holy Father had been a student at the College of the Americas where the Lord Cardinal had once been Dean. They chatted for a few minutes about old times, about walking in the Alban Hills and holidays by the lake at Castel Gandolfo. The Lord Cardinal regretted that his increasing frailty did not permit him to travel to Rome these days, but he looked forward to receiving the Holy Father when he next favoured the continent with his presence. Memories of his most recent, triumphant tour still lingered. A photograph commemorating their last encounter had pride of place on his writing desk. The Pope, smiling broadly, arm around his ancient mentor, his red cloak billowing so that it almost enveloped them.

190

No sooner had the Holy Father rung off than Father Anselm, who had doubtless been listening on the line in the ante chamber, reappeared to say that His Excellency the President for Life wished to convey his congratulations to the Lord Cardinal. 'In person.' Father Anselm's demeanour, normally tranquil, betrayed a trace of panic. 'His Excellency is on his way, *now*. Expected in the next ten minutes.' This news triggered a bout of frenetic activity from the sisters. Chairs were re-arranged, papers cleared, cushions plumped. Only the Lord Cardinal remained unfazed, gazing thoughtfully into the garden. Soon, from the distance, a wail of sirens. The chanting of the crowd, by now audible, fading as the sirens grew closer, the sound echoing around the walls of the court-yard below. Much slamming of car doors and barking of orders. Then, briefly, silence before the double doors to the Oriel Room parted to reveal, propped up on his gold-topped walking stick, the sturdy frame of His Excellency the President for Life, beaming from ear to ear. In the gloom beyond the doorway, large, unsmiling men lurked.

'Eminence.'

'Excellency.' The Lord Cardinal made to rise. Father Anselm made ready to assist.

'No, no, Eminence, please ...' Too late, the Lord Cardinal was already on his feet, hand outstretched, the emerald on the third finger of his left hand glinting in the sunlight from the window. Slowly and with a show of *faux* humility, the Life President bowed, then, taking the gnarled hand in his own, kissed the ring, waiting patiently until the Lord Cardinal had, with the assistance of Father Anselm, been lowered gently back into his seat before placing himself in the armchair opposite.

Shorn of uniform and the dark glasses that he habitually wore in public, the Life President cut a deceptively jovial figure. A good head of greying hair, perhaps a little red in the face (high blood pressure?), overweight, but not excessively so for a man whose lifestyle was sedentary. The walking stick and a downward curve of the left side of his mouth the only evidence of the stroke His Excellency was rumoured to have suffered some months previously. Over the many years they had been acquainted, the Lord Cardinal had noted with disappointment that the Life President's charm belied what went on in his dungeons.

'Forgive me, Eminence, for the short notice of my visit ...' In truth the Life President's movements were never communicated in advance, not even to his closest associates. In fact, *especially* not to his closest associates. Not since a car bomb had detonated five years ago, killing three bodyguards and a dozen bystanders, but mercifully (or regrettably, depending on your point of view) leaving the Life President unscathed. Inevitably the incident, one of at least half a dozen assassination attempts that had marred His Excellency's long reign, was ascribed to *Los Banditos*, but those who knew about such matters whispered that the explosive device was well beyond the technical prowess (not to say the competence) of the ragtag guerrillas, whose sphere of influence was confined mainly to the rainforests of the south. The suspicion was that the source of the explosion was somewhat closer to home than could be publicly admitted. Of course, such specious rumours were roundly excoriated in the official media and those propagating them were threatened with arrest, but it was noticed that within a week the interior minister, the chief of the armed forces, three generals and an unspecified number of officers of lower rank had disappeared from public life. Some, indeed, had vanished altogether.

'. . . but I felt compelled, on so auspicious a day, to convey in person to your Eminence my esteem and that of all our people . . .' Just what, wondered the Lord Cardinal, entitles this oaf to speak for the people? It was almost thirty years since the people had been consulted about anything and, even then, the ballot had been shamelessly rigged. But no matter. This was not a day for quibbling.

'Your Excellency is most kind.'

'. . . Of course, I realise that over the years we have had

our, er, differences.' Differences? That was one way of putting it. There was the little matter of the priest and four nuns whose bodies had been found in shallow graves on wasteland a few miles from the capital. Needless to say, that atrocity, too, had been attributed to *Los Banditos*, but why would the guerrillas wish to murder five humble souls who had devoted their lives to helping the impoverished? Then there was the Bishop of Santa Maria Madre de Dios, an outspoken critic of the regime, gunned down in his own cathedral. That was ascribed to renegade soldiers, acting strictly on their own initiative. Three men had been swiftly arrested and imprisoned in the central barracks, but within weeks they were said to be back in circulation. Twice in bygone years the Lord Cardinal had had the temerity to call for free elections, but he had long ago abandoned hope that anything would change for the better during the lifetime of the present incumbent.

The Life President was in full flow. 'But today we must not dwell on such matters. Today is a day for celebration. The entire nation is rejoicing. And not just the nation, the entire Catholic world.'

'Indeed.'

'And in such good health, too. Your Eminence is an example to us all. To have lived so long, faculties intact. Still in office. Truly, a miracle.'

'It is true, the Lord has smiled upon me.'

'And upon our poor country, Eminence.' That, thought the Lord Cardinal, was a matter for debate.

The charade continued for a full ten minutes. The Life President affecting unbridled love and respect. The Lord Cardinal conceding little beyond occasionally acknowledging the torrent of courtesies. In due course the Life President rose, bowed, kissed the ring once more and limped towards the double doors, which miraculously opened at his approach. Turning, he bowed again and was gone, a wail of sirens announcing the departure of his convoy.

Within a year the Life President was dead. He was said to have died peacefully in his sleep, which caused some unkind souls to whisper that there was no justice in this world. Only among the kleptocracy was there any sign of genuine grief, although many others deemed it expedient to be seen to mourn his passing. Generally, however, grief was in short supply. The crowds that lined the street as his cortege passed were notably subdued. A message of condolence from the US president was bland. The Lord Cardinal presided at the funeral, slumped in his throne to the left of the high altar. The only heads of state in attendance were from neighbouring tyrannies. Other countries made do with ambassadors and some with a mere *charge d'affairs*.

Within hours of the Life President's demise, the chief of

the armed forces, a man with no public profile, declared himself interim head of state. This was not well received. A crowd, consisting mainly of students, gathered outside the palace chanting slogans about freedom. Such defiance was unprecedented, but the soldiers surrounding the palace made no effort to intervene. A commentator on national radio was even allowed to express the hope that some form of democracy might follow. The American ambassador was interviewed and called for stability, but he, too, hinted that the time had perhaps come for a lighter touch.

At the residence of the Lord Cardinal there was a good deal of coming and going. The US ambassador visited daily. Also, various notable civilians, such as the vice chancellor of the university and a former finance minister who, for reasons of health, had spent many years exiled in Miami, and a number of prominent businessmen, some who had supported the regime and some who had kept a discreet distance. Emissaries scurried hither and thither between the presidential palace and the residence. It was even rumoured that the cardinal was secretly in touch with the leader of *Los Banditos*. Outside, in the piazza, journalists gathered. Among them representatives of the North American television networks, who these days did not often stray far beyond Washington. Their cameras focused on the gates that led to the inner courtyard, recording every arrival and departure. Curious citizens also assembled. At first a handful, but gradually swelling in number until the square was more or less full. Day and night the vigil was maintained. Candles were lit. Prayers said. Slogans chanted. An air of expectation reigned.

Then, on the feast of the Immaculate Conception, immediately upon the expiry of the seven days of mourning decreed by the interim president, a statement was issued in the name of the Lord Cardinal announcing that at 6 p.m. precisely he would broadcast to the nation on a matter of great importance. When the moment came, the camera showed him seated at his desk in a book-lined study. Upright and magnificent in a scarlet biretta, wisps of snow-white hair protruding above his ears, gold pectoral cross glinting. Some who had seen him slumped in his throne at the funeral of his late Excellency remarked that of late the Lord Cardinal seemed to have acquired a new lease of life.

He spoke slowly, each word carefully enunciated, pausing between sentences. *'Dear Citizens, I greet you in the name of God Almighty. I am pleased to announce that, after scrupulous consultation with all interested parties, an interim government is to be formed.'* He looked straight into the camera, voice firm and clear, betraying no hint of his great age. *'It will consist of persons of unimpeachable integrity whose sole interest is the welfare of our beloved country. We are not a poor country. We are a rich country that has been grievously misgoverned. The new administration will have the lofty responsibility of preparing the way for free elections that will, under all circumstances, take place within one year from today. I have spoken with the Secretary General of the United Nations and he has agreed to send international observers to ensure the proper conduct of these elections. The first contingent will arrive next week.*

'I can further announce that our brothers, who call themselves Protectors of the Impoverished, and who for so many years have inhabited the southern jungles, have agreed an indefinite ceasefire. Two of their leaders will serve in the interim government.

'As for political prisoners, there will be a total amnesty and, in due course, a commission of inquiry to discover the fate of those who have disappeared.

'As regards membership of the interim government, a list will be published at the end of this broadcast. With great reluctance, but in response to the pleas from those who have at heart the best interests of our country, I have agreed temporarily to preside. His Holiness the Pope, to whom I have spoken within the past hour, has personally consented to this unusual arrangement. I call on every citizen, rich or poor, high or low, to play his or her part in ensuring a peaceful transition to a future that is happier than the past.

'May God bless you all, dear citizens.'

And with that, the Lord Cardinal was gone.

Of the military man who had declared himself interim president not two weeks previously, there was no mention. He melted away as swiftly as he appeared without ever having registered in the public consciousness. He was reported to have departed, at short notice, on a one-way ticket to Florida. The American ambassador had personally escorted him to the airport. 'I just said "goodbye",' he said later. 'Nothing historic, just "goodbye".'

The news of a government presided over by a prince of the church was widely reported around the world, generally with approval, though there were some who argued that, however worthy the cause, the church should not meddle in affairs of state. There was widespread astonishment at his great age, exceeding perhaps by two decades that of any other head of state. Only his late Excellency, the Life President of Malawi, Dr Hastings Kamuzu Banda, came close to matching the longevity of the Lord Cardinal, and even he had assumed office at a much younger age. As for a government presided over by a cardinal, one had to go back to Richelieu for a precedent, and that was not entirely a happy one. Briefly, the fact of a president, albeit an interim one, who was both a centenarian and a cardinal, served to focus worldwide attention on the fledgling democracy, whose only previous claim to fame had been to feature prominently in the reports of various

CHRIS MULLIN

human rights organisations. Special correspondents were dispatched from every continent to bear witness to this astonishing turn of events.

The elections went ahead as scheduled. They were contested by no less than thirty political parties, none of which had been in existence for more than a year and only half a dozen of which were rewarded with seats in the National Assembly. Unusually for elections in this part of the world, few of the losing candidates contested the outcome. The new president, elected after a run-off, was a Harvard-educated professor who had returned to serve his country after a long period of service with the International Monetary Fund. Wisely, he decided to form a government of national unity, containing representatives of all but one of the elected parties (the Socialist Workers' Party having refused to join). The new minister of foreign affairs was a female diplomat who had lived outside the country for some years, working for a think tank in Washington. The former leader of the uprising in the south, who had adapted with remark-able alacrity (too much so, in the eyes of some) to the perks of office, was appointed minister for social justice, a post he had also held in the interim government. He was one of three former *banditos* to accept ministerial office. The vice chancellor of the country's sole univer-sity was confirmed as minister of education, a post he too had held in the interim government. For the first time anyone could recall, the minister of defence was a civilian. Among the new government's first announcements, a modest (too modest some thought) programme of land reform, the construction of a new tarmacadam highway from the capital to the south of the country, and free primary education to be accompanied by a school-building programme, part-funded by an IMF loan. Also, a National Minerals Corporation was to be established to process applications from foreign oil companies for the exploitation of the oil and other minerals said to exist in large quantities in remote parts of the country. No doubt, as in other democracies, disappointment and squabbling would soon set in, but for the time being an air of optimism prevailed as this small country, once a pariah among nation states, basked in unprecedented international goodwill.

As for the Lord Cardinal, after handing over the seals of office to his duly anointed successor at a ceremony conducted, in deference to his great age, at his residence, he disappeared from public view. On the rare occasions he was glimpsed in the garden, he was by now confined to a wheelchair, though his intellect was said to be as acute as ever. Although he had done his best to discourage the practice, his photograph had replaced those of the late President for Life in homes and businesses the length and breadth of the country. In years to come busts and statues would appear in public spaces throughout the land, the largest and most impressive of which was installed in the square opposite his official residence, where the faithful (and, on occasion, the not so faithful) had once gathered to receive his blessing.

On the last day of his life, shortly after his one hundred and third birthday, the Lord Cardinal was roused as usual before dawn and helped to dress by Father Anselm, who then wheeled him down the corridor to the chapel. As usual he took breakfast in his armchair by the window of the Oriel Room, after which Father Anselm read aloud a passage from the scriptures. As was his habit, he listened to the morning news on a radio nearly as ancient as he. The main story, a report that bodies had been found in a mass grave at a remote hacienda, just another chapter in the unravelling legacy of his late Excellency. Afterwards he dozed lightly. These days sleep increasingly consumed his daylight hours.

At noon, when Father Anselm next looked in on him, everything was as it had always been. Pedro was pottering in the garden. Spray from the sprinklers on the lawn sparkled in the sunshine. Beyond, a view of the glittering ocean. On the table by his armchair, a tumbler of water, untouched. Gold-rimmed spectacles hung loose about his neck. On the Lord Cardinal's lap, a half-folded letter in the hand of the Holy Father himself, offering warmest congratulations on the successful completion of his life's mission, wishing him a peaceful retirement and assuring him they would meet again in paradise, if not before.

THE MAN WHO SHOT
THE PRESIDENT

When you have killed the president of the United States and got clean away, life does not have much more to offer in the way of highs. Yeah, I was there. On the sixth floor of the Texas Book Depository. It was I, not Oswald, who fired the fatal shot. Just like he said, Oswald was a patsy. Used to smuggle in the rifle. That's all. He wasn't even there when the shooting happened. It was me. I am the one. The man who killed the president. Quite a secret to carry through life. As the years pass, the burden gets heavier, but there's no one I can tell. *No one.* In all these years I haven't uttered a word on the subject. Heard plenty of folk talking about it, but I just kept schtum. I was responsible for one of the greatest events of the twentieth century. And no one, not one single solitary human being any place on this planet, knows. Except me. Oh, and of course my partners in crime, but they are long gone. Only I survive. And that won't be for much longer.

Of course, I wasn't alone. All that lone nut stuff is crap. A job like that requires careful planning. Teamwork. On the day there were four of us. Two shooters, two drivers. Yes, there was a shooter on the grassy knoll, just like some folks claimed at the time. If you look closely at the Zapruder film, you can just about make him out. We all carried passes identifying us as Secret Service agents. Fortunately, I didn't have to show mine. Four shots, three on target, but mine's the one that blew out his brains. Took the powers-that-be another fifteen years to figure out there was a fourth shot, but by then the trail was ice cold. Four shots. They should have figured it at the time, instead of all that magic bullet shit that Warren came out with. If you ask me, they knew it wasn't Oswald, but didn't want to face the truth.

I was up there for a good three hours before the motorcade appeared. Oswald was an employee of the book depository. That gave him access. The rifle was wrapped in brown paper. He told anyone who asked that it was curtain rods. Curtain rods, my ass. He simply carried the package up to the sixth floor and left it for me by the window. Then he skedaddled. I never even set eyes on him. The plan was that he'd rendezvous in the picture house on 10th Street with a courier, but that went ape shit after the courier had a run-in with that cop – what was his name? Tip-something … Officer Tippit. Yeah, that's it. Unlucky guy, that cop. I guess he was what these days they call collateral damage. Anyway, when the cops raided the cinema, they found Oswald, but missed the courier.

Oswald thought he was in for a big payoff, but that wasn't the plan at all. He wasn't meant to survive. None of us were. They would have done me, too, except that I, alone, outwitted them. The rifle was Oswald's, purchased by mail order. He used a phoney name, but it didn't fool no one for more than about five minutes. Anyway, his fingerprints were all over it. There was even a photograph of him with it that came to light afterwards. Me? I wore latex gloves which I disposed of in a trash can on the way out of town. No way they could have let him live. No, sir. He couldn't be left to shoot his mouth off. I reckon that courier was under instructions to put a bullet in his head at the earliest opportunity and dress it up to look like suicide. When the Dallas cops got their hands on him first, he had to be silenced. A dicey moment, that. For a few hours it looked as if it might all unravel. That's when Jack Ruby stepped up to the plate. You've got to hand it to old Jack. He certainly put his life on the line. And he paid a price. All that time on death row and then cancer. I wouldn't wish that on anyone. And in all those years he never blabbed. There must have been a few big men out there biting their nails for fear of Ruby talking, but he never did. Not that he knew the whole story, anyway. None of us did.

* * *

I expect you're wondering how I ever got mixed up in all this. Korea's where it began. I volunteered for the Marine Corp and, after basic training in Quantico, Virginia, was shipped to Korea. That would be in September '50.

The North Koreans had overrun the south and we were helping to push them back. We landed at Inchon and fought our way to Seoul. Jesus, what a mess. The whole fucking place had been destroyed. I've never seen destruction like that. In some towns, not a single intact building. Nothing but mud and muck and refugees living in the rubble. Eventually we got into the north, almost to the Yalu River. Then the Chinese came in and, man, did we hammer them, but they just kept coming, wave after wave. It went on for months until eventually we found ourselves back at the dividing line between north and south. After that, stalemate. Me? I was a sniper. One of an elite little unit. Yup. Now you see where this is heading, don't you?

My job was to sit quietly in the ruins and take out anyone one on the other side who came into my sights. It required patience. Sometimes I'd wait days, holed up in some heap of rubble in the middle of no-man's land, waiting for some unsuspecting Chink to stick his head above the parapet. And then *bang*. Just one shot. Never a second. Otherwise they'd know where it came from. Then head down and wait, wait until darkness and then hightail out of there back to our own lines. At that point, of course, there was always a risk of being taken out by your own side. That's what happened to a lot of our guys. Gunned down by the trigger-happy morons on our side. Friendly fire they call it, don't they? Of course, they never put that in the telegram they send home. 'Died in action, bravely facing the enemy.' Or some such shit. Nobody ever officially dies of friendly fire.

To be honest, I didn't think I'd make it out of there. About half my unit didn't. The casualty rate for snipers is high, but there is a certain job satisfaction. By my reckoning I scored seventeen hits, including several officers. That was the highest in my unit. Several of us – yeah, me included – were awarded Purple Hearts and a handshake from the president. Ironic, isn't it? In view of what came later.

* * *

My dear old mom idolised the Kennedys. Jesus, she'd be turning in her grave if she'd known what her Number One Son had done. We were never that close, not after Korea.

After I came home she used to say she didn't recognise me any more, compared to the nice, sweet, compliant little boy she used to know before I went away. And it's true, that damn war destroyed my soul. All that destruction, all that killing, it kinda numbed me. Not that I took to drink and drugs or anything. Not like some of them. Just that I was dead inside. And it must have showed.

After discharge, I got a job in a warehouse. Lasted about nine months, until I got into a fight with the foreman. After that I drifted. In and out of work. In and out of doss houses. Even did a bit of lumberjacking in Canada. Went home about once a year to see my mom. My dad died soon after I came back from Korea and she was mostly on her own after that. Except for my sister who lived on the other side of town. I had a brother, too, but he turned into a bad 'un and ended up in jail. Not that I can talk, 'cos no one turned out to be a bigger badass than me. Better not say any more about my family or where I came from 'cos I don't want to cause them no bother, if by any remote chance word gets out.

Late '50s I went into private security. One of my old buddies from Korea put me on to it. Looking after bullion, VIPs, that sort of shit. Took care of Sinatra once. Not a nice man. And Bob Hope. Not so keen on him either. Although, truthfully, I enjoyed the work. Good money, no shortage of clients, some very generous. Marines apart, that was the nearest I came to stable employment in my whole life. Looking back, it was also when I was happiest. Settled down with a woman. A nice girl, from Arkansas. A natural blonde, ten years my junior. For a while we went everywhere together. Introduced me to her folks and all that. Even took a little holiday in Europe. We were together about eighteen months, but it never quite worked out. I guess she looked into my soul and saw there was nothing there. Then one day there was a knock on the door. Another of my pals from Korea. He'd worn well, all things considered. Lean and fit, thinning hair, same dead eyes as we all seem to have acquired out there. He didn't beat about the bush.

'Hey, old buddy, how do you fancy earning some real money?'

'Doing what?'

'Remember what we were up to in Korea?'

'How could I forget?'

'That sort of thing.'

'Sniping, you mean?'

'Nothing illegal. Totally legit. We'll be working for the government. Taking out America's enemies. Totally classified, of course. Not a word to anyone. Ever.'

And that, my friends, was the beginning of the long road that ended in Dealey Plaza, Dallas.

* * *

There were half a dozen of us. All Korea vets. Sworn to secrecy. Given pseudonyms and told never to disclose our real names, even to each other. The only one I recognised was the man who got me into this. First, there was a little refresher course. Somewhere in Colorado. There were other guys being trained there. Foreigners, mostly. Tibetans, so it was rumoured, being prepared for infiltration back into China. Later, there were Latinos. Cubans, I guess. Hill tribesmen from northern Laos and southern China. The United States government was into some weird shit at that time. Anyway, we were kept well apart. Confined to a little compound within a compound, except for the occasional early morning run and use of the shooting range when the others weren't about. There were courses in unarmed combat, we polished up our shooting skills, practised the art of disguise, learned about radio transmission and how to resist interrogation in the event of capture. One of the guys dropped out in the early stages, but the rest us of graduated, if that's the right word.

Our first job was in Panama, dealing with some very bad dudes who were smuggling cocaine into the US and slicing up anyone who got in the way. No qualms about that. There was talk of being sent to Cuba to take out Castro, but nothing ever came of that. Later, we were sent to the Dominican Republic disguised as businessmen. Smart suits, Rolex watches, a luxury villa on the edge of the capital. Our mission was to take out Trujillo, the head honcho, another very bad man, but his own guys got to him before we did. That was in May '61. There were other missions, too, but I wasn't party to them all. Years later, in the '70s, when Congress started probing and people in high places started publishing their memoirs, I heard that some guy called Harvey in the CIA had set up a programme called 'executive action'. For the assassination of foreign leaders. No one ever told me, but I guess we were part of that. Apparently Kennedy found out about it and quietly closed it down, which earned him a few more enemies than he already had. After Trujillo, things went quiet. We were paid off and sent back to civilian life to await further instructions. It was another two years or more before anyone got in touch. Fourteen November 1963, to be exact.

* * *

As I said, my mother worshipped the Kennedys, especially Jackie. It wasn't so much the politics – Mom wasn't much into politics – just the glamour. 'My, that girl is so beautiful ...' she used to say, '... and those children.' She had a picture of the Kennedys on the sideboard, alongside her own family. After Dallas, I only went home once. Ma was devastated about what happened. She'd gone right overboard. Erected a pole in the garden with a flag that remained at half-mast for months. As if that weren't enough, she was keeping a fucking scrapbook. All the magazines piled on a table in the living room with bits cut out of them. Pictures of Jackie and the children. The photo on the sideboard draped in black. Imagine how I felt. 'Jesus, Ma, can't you talk about something else?' But she couldn't. On and on she went. Tears in her eyes. It was driving my sister mad. In the end I couldn't take it anymore. I stayed two nights and then drove away. Sent flowers on her birthday, the occasional postcard, but the next time I set eyes on her she was in her coffin.

* * *

I guess you are wondering who set this up. Me too. I think about it more and more. At the time, I thought I knew, but as the years have passed a thick fog has descended. There have been a lot of theories. Miami Cubans, Castro Cubans, the Russians, the mob or even some agency of the US government. All I know is that one day when I was minding my own business, scraping a living back in private security, a man turned up at my lodgings. Well built, white, about six two, a tattoo on his neck, under

214

his left ear. Ex-military, special forces, if I were to guess. It was evening, the light was fading. He didn't introduce himself. Just took me for a stroll by the canal and asked if I was interested in one last assignment. Big money, he said. So much that I would never have to work again. Didn't specify the target, only that this would be bigger than anything I'd ever done in my life and that, after it was over, I would need to change my identity and lie low for some time, years maybe. But not to worry, 'cos I'd be well looked after. Not having anything better to do (work had slacked off a bit since the early days), I said 'yes'. At which point he shook my hand, nice firm handshake, and said I'd be hearing from him again soon. He reappeared three days later, just pulled up beside me in a big old Cadillac and told me to get in. Next thing I know we're in some sort of villa on the outskirts of Houston. High walls. Entry phone. A derelict fountain in the courtyard, with just a muddy puddle in the basin. Four of us. One guy I knew from that operation in Dominica and our two minders, unsmiling gringos, leather gloves, dark glasses, sharp suits, polished shoes. Cartons of orange juice on the sideboard. Sandwiches still in their wrappings, a few pastries. A jug of coffee bubbling away. We waited five, maybe ten minutes. Then a guy comes in. A big brute of a fellow. Shaved head. Prominent cheekbones. Black moustache. No pleasantries. All business. Resembled one of them bully sergeants I knew in the marines. 'There will be four of you,' he said. 'Two drivers,' he indicated the gringos still wearing their gloves and dark glasses, standing slightly apart. 'And two shooters,' nodding to me and my one-time colleague. 'The weapons will be Carcanos with telescopic lenses, range 1,000 metres, six rounds per clip. One clip should be enough. You won't have time to reload. I understand you are familiar with these weapons. That right?'

Our turn to nod.

'Yes, sir.'

To be honest, the Carcano wouldn't have been my weapon of choice, but I was not inclined to argue and, anyway, I had used one before. The US market was flooded with them after the Italian army replaced them with something more up to date.

'You'll get a chance to practice with your weapon later today and then you won't see it again until it's time to use it for real. You won't have to carry it to your vantage point. Someone else will do that.' The target is a single, high-value individual in an open-topped vehicle, likely to be moving at between ten and fifteen miles an hour. The plan is to hit him from two sides. One shooter in front; the other behind, up high somewhere.'

'Open-topped vehicle'. That's when the dime ought to have dropped, but believe it or not neither of us twigged. Truth to tell, I didn't even know Kennedy was coming to Texas, such was the air pocket of ignorance in which I lived. If I'd known it was Kennedy, I'd have made my excuses and left. Or, more likely, I would have nodded in the right places and then quietly disappeared. Wouldn't have fancied telling those guys to their faces what they didn't want to hear.

The house didn't look lived in. Threadbare carpets. A few sticks of furniture. Half a dozen wooden chairs around a scratchy old dining table, empty bookshelves and a sideboard with the sandwiches. Marks on the wall where pictures had been hung. Come to think of it, there was a 'For Sale' board outside by the front gate. There were other people in the house. We heard them coming and going. Didn't catch sight of anyone, but I reckon we were being observed. There was some sort of spy hole in the door that led into the next room, and if you looked carefully, you could see the light behind it change, as though someone was there, moving, whispering occasionally.

'Questions, gentlemen.'

'Yes, sir,' said my Dominica buddy. 'If this is such a big deal, aren't we going to need new identities, driving licences, bank accounts and all that shit?'

'The intention is, gentlemen, that after this is over you will go home and carry on with your lives for the foreseeable future. Today you will receive a substantial down payment in cash and in due course large sums will be paid into bank accounts, which will be set up for you in Panama, the Caymans. Or perhaps in Europe. You will be notified of the details in due course. You will need new identities to access these.'

You may find it a mite strange, our lack of curiosity about the identity of the target, but that was normal in our line of business. The less you knew, the longer you lived. Anyway, we'd find out soon enough.

I had a question, too. 'Sir, if we're going to need knew identities, passports, driving licence and all that, might there not be some formalities to complete?'

'Don't you worry about that, son. That's all taken care of.' The subject was never mentioned again. At the time I didn't think much about this. It was only when I reflected that it dawned on me that all that stuff about bank accounts and new identities was a load of hooey, because we weren't supposed to survive. I kept this thought to myself, but I also began to take precautions.

Later that day, we were taken out to a farm in the middle of nowhere and given our Carcanos and a pile of ammo clips. We spent a couple of hours practice-shooting tins off fences, blasting apart gourds hanging from trees, and finally we were taken high into a barn roof and told to shoot at some kind of mechanical contraption attached to a wire which was intended to simulate a moving vehicle. Easy stuff. We passed with flying colours. Sometime that afternoon a man with a camera and a big flash came and took mugshots. 'For your new passports,' he told us. My spirits lifted a little at that point. Maybe we were going to survive after all.

When that was done, the rifles and the remaining ammo clips were collected up and we were each handed a leather attaché case which we were instructed not to open until we got home. Mine contained cash in used hundred-dollar bills bound together with elastic bands. More money than I had ever seen. Enough to open a small business, maybe buy a little house in some town in the middle of nowhere and settle back into a normal life. Except, of course, that after this there would never again be anything normal about my life.

* * *

Do I regret what happened? Sure as hell I do. There isn't a day when I don't think about it. If I had my time over again, I would have led a completely different life. Never have volunteered for that darn sniper unit in Korea. Gone home and got a trade like my old man. Settled down in some small Midwest town with a wife and two kids. Brought them up decently. Baseball, soccer, just like normal dads. Gone drinking with my buddies. The older I get the more it haunts me, but I try not to dwell. What's done is done. There ain't no going back. In Korea we never had to engage with consequences. We never thought of the other side as boys with moms and dads and brothers and sisters, like us. To us they were just Chinks, and there were lots more where they came from. Anyway, we never had to look them in the eyes. One fleeting glimpse and *bang*, they were gone. In Panama we were dealing with the worst type of gangsters, real bad hats. Taking them out was a public service. I felt good about that. But that Kennedy. He was something else altogether. Whether you liked him or not, everyone in America, everyone in the whole world, knew Kennedy. We'd all looked into his eyes. We knew everything about him. Well, not quite everything. All that stuff with the women came out later. We knew about his wife, his children, his father – Old Joe. We'd heard him give speeches to adoring crowds. The Kennedys were royalty. American royalty. Something we'd never had before or since. To be honest, I had nothing against Kennedy. He'd never done me no harm. To be sure, he'd made a few enemies. Those Miami Cubans, gangsters many of them. And his brother, Bobby, was going after the mob. But I didn't know anyone who hated him enough to want him dead. At least not until I got mixed up in that awful bad business in Dallas.

* * *

After our day in Houston I was taken home by one of the gringos. Little or no conversation. 'Someone will come for you in the next few days. Be ready. Pack yourself an overnight bag. Now get your ass outta here.' That was just about all he had to say. This must have been about 18 November. The clock was ticking. As yet no one had even mentioned Dallas. If they had, I might have put two and two together.

They came back for me early on the morning of the twenty-first. Same car, same gringo. Same lack of information.

'Where are we going?'

'Somewhere.'

I doubt he uttered more than half a dozen sentences during the entire journey and those were about the price of petrol, food and the weather. Each item preceded by the f-word.

We drove for four hours. It soon became apparent we were headed for Dallas, but even now it hadn't occurred to me why. We were taken to a house a mile or so from downtown. Like the villa in Houston it seemed only to be temporarily occupied. It also had an entry phone and a high wall. Sergeant Psycho was waiting for us in a back room, but there were other people this time. Three men in overcoats and trilbies hovered in the shadows. On their way out as we came in. Looked like they'd just broken up from some meeting. Uneasy, pulling their hats down, like they didn't want us to see them. It wasn't until I saw that clip of Jack Ruby shooting Oswald that I realised where I'd seen him before.

On the table a large-scale, hand-drawn diagram of Dealey Plaza. A red dotted line leading from the direction of the airport, through downtown into Elm Street. The book depository was marked with a red cross. Likewise, the patch of land that would later become known as the grassy knoll. Also the triple flyover that carried the railroad over Elm Street. Maybe the original intention was to have a shooter on the overpass. If so, they had changed their plan. A copy of the *Dallas Morning News* lay unopened on a chair. The front page was all about Kennedy. So that was it. Kennedy was coming. It was only then that I finally figured it out. Jesus effing Christ. The blood drained from my face. I swallowed hard.

'Well, gentlemen, you've figured it, I guess.' My companion nodded. In all that time we'd hardly exchanged a word. Maybe he'd known all along, but I sure as hell hadn't.

'Is that a problem?'

The question was directed at me.

The slightest hesitation and then, 'No, sir.'

From that moment my fate and that of the thirty-fifth president of the United States were sealed. The odd thing was that, within my hearing, no one at any time referred to the president by his name. Nor did anyone mention the office he held. To everyone present in that room he was known simply as 'the target'.

* * *

The briefing lasted little more than an hour. They had thought it all out. They had diagrams and photographs. They even knew which vehicle the president would be travelling in. I reckon they had someone on the inside. The motorcade would emerge from behind the court house, swing sharp right into Houston Street and then, after a couple of hundred yards, left into Elm Street. There would be a clear line of sight from both the book depository and the stockade. 'That is when you hit him.'

'How can you be sure of the route?'

'Because, gentleman, it's all over the frigging newspapers.' He held up the *Morning Post* and, sure enough, there was a map.

'How do we get away after the event?'

'I am coming to that'. Sergeant Psycho was eerily calm. Nothing in his demeanour betrayed the enormity of the project. Appearances can be deceptive. He was officer material, not a sergeant.

'There is a parking lot behind the book depository.

There will be two cars. Carlos and Marco,' he indicated the drivers, 'will be waiting for you there'. That was the first and last time anyone was referred to by name, if indeed those were their names. 'All of you will be carrying Secret Service ID. Don't use it unless you have to.'

We tossed a silver dollar to see who went where. My companion chose the stockade. I guess he felt that would make for an easier getaway. As it turned out, he was wrong. That left me with the depository.

Dinner was served. Steak and fries, mustard, ketchup. Generous helpings, but strictly no alcohol. It was served by a nervous, dark-skinned Hispanic woman who kept her head down and her mouth shut. She just laid out the plates and fled. Then we were shown to an upstairs room, empty except for a couple of mattresses and two sleeping bags. My companion slept like a log. I doubt I slept a wink. Breakfast – orange juice, coffee, eggs, bacon and hash browns – was on the table. It was still dark outside. The table was cleared by the same nervous young woman and then it was down to business. So far as I could tell we were alone in the house now, apart from the gringo drivers and Sergeant Psycho. Or perhaps I should call him Captain Psycho. That dude was definitely officer material.

* * *

Looking back, I am surprised how easy it was. By nine, I was in position. No one challenged me. If they had, I'd have used the Secret Service pass with which we had been issued that morning. The place was humming. So far as many Texans were concerned, 22 November 1963 was just another working day. I took a service lift to the sixth floor. There were a couple of other guys with a trolley in there, but they got out lower down. The sixth floor was deserted, some sort of storage depot piled high with boxes. The Carcano was exactly where they said it would be, leaning against a pile of boxes by the first window, wrapped in brown paper. Good old Lee – not that I or anyone else for that matter had ever heard of him at that time – had done his job. By nightfall he would be one of the most famous people in the world and I would remain unknown, unheard of, for the rest of my days. I built myself a little den among the boxes. They were heavy, filled with school books. I piled them so high that even if someone had come in they wouldn't have seen me, but no one came up there all morning. I was completely alone. I checked the gun was loaded and aimed it out of the window a couple of times, lining up the shot. Someone down in the Plaza spotted it and pointed up at the window. I held my breath, but nothing came of it. I settled down for a long wait, half hoping that there would be a last-minute change of route and that I would never be put to the test, but to my infinite, everlasting regret everything went exactly according to plan.

* * *

You may wonder how I got out of there alive. And why I am still alive today. That's because I had a plan. There was no way I was going to get back into the car with that gringo. Instead I had taken the precaution of stashing a bag full of money, along with my passport, driving licence, a couple of changes of clothes and toiletries in a locker in the bus station at Fort Worth. All I had to do was double back, collect and disappear. When it was over, I got up, leaned the rifle against the window, removed the latex gloves, stuffed them in the pocket of my pants and took the stairs to the ground floor. There was a lot of screaming and shouting, people were flowing down the stairwell from other floors. I just went with the flow. Outside there was mayhem. The motorcade had long gone, but people were running round in circles, hollering and weeping. Several were pointing up at the sixth floor from where only minutes ago I had fired the fatal shot. A couple of patrol men, guns drawn, raced past and into the building. Me? I just kept going, jogging down Elm Street to the Greyhound station. From there I caught the first bus out of town. It departed on time, about five minutes after

I boarded. No road blocks, no searches, nothing. No one paid me the slightest heed. The traffic was light and we cleared the city in about twenty minutes. There were few signs that this was no ordinary day. Cop cars, blue lights flashing, sirens wailing, headed in the other direction, but I guess you can see that most days in a city like Dallas. We passed a shopping mall where people were gathered around a store window full of televisions, but that apart there was no sign that this day was different from any other. We had just cleared the city limits when the driver announced over the intercom that Kennedy was dead. I guess I was the only person on that bus to whom the news didn't come as a surprise.

***

PRIORITY FLASH

1715 HRS

011879

EX MARTIN,

PRO COLBY

ATTACHED TRANSCRIPT OF TAPE FOUND ON BODY OF UNIDENTIFIED MALE LIVING REMOTE VILLAGE IN ITALIAN ALPS STOP DEAD SOME DAYS STOP APPEARS DIED FROM BARBITURATE OVERDOSE STOP IN POSSESSION OF BRITISH

PASSPORT NUMBER 379540A STOP IN NAME OF CHRISTOPHER JOHN FIELDING STOP REPORTED STOLEN IN ROME TWO YEARS AGO STOP DECEASED BELIEVED BY LOCAL RESIDENTS TO BE AN AMERICAN STOP SEARCH OF PROPERTY HAS FAILED TO UNEARTH ANY CLUES AS TO IDENTITY OF DECEASED STOP AWAITING YR INSTRUCTIONS STOP

PRIORITY FLASH
1900 HRS
011879
EX COLBY
PRO MARTIN
BAG TAPE AND ALL, RPT ALL, COPIES OF TRANSCRIPT TO LANGLEY MARKED DIRECTOR STOP EYES ONLY STOP

Note 1: On Saturday, April 27, 1996, former CIA director William Colby was found floating face down in the Wicomico river, near his holiday home in Maryland.

Note 2: Above are the contents of a file that, in November 2023, was discovered buried deep in the basement of CIA headquarters at Langley, Virginia, by an academic who had been commissioned to write an official history of the Agency. Scrawled in felt tip pen across the cover, in what appears to be the hand of Director Colby, is the single word, underlined three times, 'BURN'. But for reasons unknown his instruction does not appear to have been obeyed.